"Who said I was a maiden?" Gabby closed her eyes for a second, allowing the sun to wash over her face, the corners of her lips curving up slightly into a smile.

"You didn't have to say it," Alessandro said. "I could feel it in your kiss." Or rather, the lack of it.

Her stomach sank down to her toes and she opened her eyes again, the corners of her lips falling. "Was it so terrible?"

Of course it hadn't been.

"Not terrible. Inexperienced. I could taste it on your skin."

"That's ridiculous. Inexperience doesn't have a flavor."

He grabbed hold of her arm again, turned her to face him, drawing her closely toward him. Rather than speeding up, this time her heart stopped beating altogether. He lowered his head slightly, then reached up, sliding his thumb along the edge of her lip. "Yes, Gabriella, inexperience absolutely has a flavor. And on your lips, there was also innocence and wildflowers. I did not mistake the taste of any of that."

The Billionaire's Legacy

A search for truth and the promise of passion!

For nearly sixty years, Italian billionaire Giovanni Di Sione has kept a shocking secret. Now, nearing the end of his days, he wants his grandchildren to know their true heritage.

He sends them each on a journey to find his "Lost Mistresses," a collection of love tokens—the only remaining evidence of his lost identity, his lost history...his lost love.

With each item collected, the Di Sione siblings take one step closer to the truth... and embark on a passionate journey that none could have expected!

Find out what happens in

The Billionaire's Legacy

Di Sione's Innocent Conquest by Carol Marinelli

The Di Sione Secret Baby by Maya Blake

To Blackmail a Di Sione by Rachael Thomas

The Return of the Di Sione Wife by Caitlin Crews

Di Sione's Virgin Mistress by Sharon Kendrick

A Di Sione for the Greek's Pleasure by Kate Hewitt

A Deal for the Di Sione Ring by Jennifer Hayward

The Last Di Sione Claims His Prize by Maisey Yates

Collect all 8 volumes!

Maisey Yates

THE LAST DI SIONE CLAIMS HIS PRIZE

HARLEQUIN PRESENTS®

ISBN-13: 978-0-373-06037-5

The Last Di Sione Claims His Prize

First North American publication 2017

Special thanks and acknowledgment are given to Maisey Yates for her contribution to The Billionaire's Legacy series.

This edition published by arrangement with Harlequin Books S.A.

For questions and comments about the quality of this book, please contact us at CustomerService@Harlequin.com.

HARLEQUIN®
™ www.Harlequin.com

Printed in U.S.A.

Maisey Yates is a *New York Times* bestselling author of more than thirty romance novels. She has a coffee habit she has no interest in kicking, and a slight Pinterest addiction. She lives with her husband and children in the Pacific Northwest. When Maisey isn't writing she can be found singing in the grocery store, shopping for shoes online and probably not doing dishes. Check out her website, maiseyyates.com.

Books by Maisey Yates

Harlequin Presents

Carides's Forgotten Wife
Bound to the Warrior King
His Diamond of Convenience
To Defy a Sheikh
One Night to Risk it All

Heirs Before Vows

The Prince's Pregnant Mistress
The Spaniard's Pregnant Bride
The Italian's Pregnant Virgin

The Chatsfield

Sheikh's Desert Duty

One Night With Consequences

The Greek's Nine-Month Redemption
Married for Amari's Heir

Princes of Petras

A Christmas Vow of Seduction
The Queen's New Year Secret

Secret Heirs of Powerful Men

Heir to a Desert Legacy
Heir to a Dark Inheritance

Visit the Author Profile page at Harlequin.com for more titles.

To the authors that have brought me countless hours of reading pleasure. You inspire me.

CHAPTER ONE

IT WAS RUMORED that Alessandro Di Sione had once fired an employee for bringing his coffee back two minutes later than commanded and five degrees cooler than ordered. It was rumored that he had once released a long-term mistress with a wave of his hand and an order to collect a parting gift from his assistant in the following weeks.

There were also rumors that he breathed fire, slept in a dungeon and derived sustenance from the souls of the damned.

So, when his shiny new temporary assistant scurried into the room, with red cheeks and an apologetic expression, on the heels of his grandfather—who appeared neither red-cheeked nor sorry for anything—it was no surprise that she looked as though she was headed for the gallows.

Of course, no one denied Giovanni Di Sione entry to any place he wished to inhabit. No personal assistant, no matter how formidable, would have been able to keep his grandfather out. Age and severely reduced health notwithstanding.

But as his typical assistant was on maternity leave and her replacement had only been here for a couple of weeks, she didn't know that. She was, of course, afraid that Giovanni was an intruder and that she would be punished for the breach of security.

He saw no point in disabusing her of that notion. It was entirely possible she would spend the rest of the day deconstructing the meaning to his every glance in her direction. Likely, in the retelling, she would talk about the blackness of his eyes being a reflection of his soul, or some other such nonsense. And so, his reputation would darken even more, without him lifting a finger.

"I'm very sorry, Mr. Di Sione," she said, clearly out of breath, one palm pressed tightly over her rather unimpressive breasts.

He made a low, disapproving sound and raised one dark brow.

She was trembling now. Like a very small dog. "Should I go back to work, sir?" she asked, nervous eyes darting toward the door.

He waved his hand and she scurried back out much the same as she had scurried in.

"I see you're up and moving around," Alex said, not descending into sentimentality because his relationship with Giovanni didn't allow for that. With each returned Lost Mistress, Giovanni's health had recovered bit by bit.

"It's been a while since my last treatment, so I'm feeling better."

"Good to hear it."

"The way you acted toward your assistant was not

overly kind, Alessandro," his grandfather said, taking the seat in front of Alex's desk somewhat shakily.

"You say that as though you believe I have a concern about being perceived as kind. We both know I do not."

"Yes, but I also know you're not as terrible as you pretend to be." Giovanni leaned back in his chair, both hands planted on his knees. He was getting on in years and, after seventeen years in remission, his leukemia had returned. At ninety-eight, Giovanni likely didn't have many years left on the earth regardless of his health, but it had certainly added a bit of urgency to the timeline.

The goal being to recover each and every one of Giovanni's Lost Mistresses. Stories of these treasures were woven into Alex's consciousness. His grandfather had been spinning tales about them from the time Alessandro was a boy. And now, he had tasked each of his grandchildren with finding one of those lost treasures.

Except for Alex.

He had been expecting this. Waiting for quite some time to hear about what part he might play in this quest.

"Maybe not," Alex said, leaning back in his chair, unconsciously mimicking his grandfather's position.

"At least you do not dare to behave terribly in my presence."

"What can I say, *Nonno*? You are perhaps the only man on earth more formidable than I."

Giovanni waved his hand as if dismissing Alex's words. "Flattery is not the way with me, Alessandro, as you well know."

He did know. His grandfather was a man of business. A man who had built a life out of nothing upon his arrival to America, a man who understood commerce. He had instilled that in Alex. It was how they connected. Where their minds met.

"Don't tell me you're feeling bored and you wanted to get your hands back into the shipping business?"

"Not at all. But I do have a job for you."

Alex nodded slowly. "Is it my time to take a mistress?"

"I have saved the last one for you, Alessandro. The painting."

"Painting?" Alex lifted a paperweight from his desk and moved it, tapping the glass with his index finger. "Don't tell me you were a great collector of clowns on velvet or some such."

Giovanni chuckled. "No. Nothing of the kind. I'm looking for *The Lost Love*."

Alex frowned. "My art history is a little bit faint at my advanced age, but the name does sound familiar."

"It should. What do you know about the disgraced royal family of Isolo D'Oro?"

"Had I known there would be a test, I would have studied before your arrival."

"You were given a very expensive education at a very high-end boarding school. I would hate to think my money was wasted."

Alex shifted, his hands still curled around the paperweight. "A school filled with teenage boys halfway across the world from their parents and very near a school filled entirely with teenage girls in the same situation. What is it you think we were studying?"

"This subject would have been *related* to your particular field of study. *The Lost Love* is a very scandalous piece of royal history. Though it was only a rumor. No one has ever seen it."

"Except for you, I take it."

"I am one of the few who can confirm its existence."

"You are ever a man of unfathomable depths."

Giovanni chuckled, inclining his head. "I am, it's true. But then, that should be a perk of living a life as long as mine. You ought to have depths and secret scandalous paintings in your past, don't you think?"

"I wouldn't know. My life primarily consists of long hours in the office."

"A waste of youth and virility in my opinion."

It was Alex's turn to laugh. "Right. Because you did not spend your thirties deeply entrenched in building your fortune."

"It is a privilege of the elderly to see things in hindsight no one can see in the present, and attempt to educate the young with that hindsight."

"I imagine it's the privilege of the young to ignore that advice?"

"Perhaps. But in this, you will listen to me. I want that painting. It is my last Lost Mistress. *My* lost love."

Alex looked at the old man, the only father figure he'd ever truly possessed. Giovanni had been the one to instill in Alex a true sense of work ethic. Of pride. Giovanni had raised him and his siblings differently than their parents had. After their deaths he had taken them in, had given them so much more than a life of instability and neglect. He had taught them to take pride in their family name, to take nothing for granted.

His son might have been a useless, debauched partyer, but Giovanni had more than made up for mistakes he made with him when he had assumed the job of raising his grandchildren.

"And you intend to send me after it?"

"Yes. I do. You spend too much time at work. Think of it as a boy's adventure. A quest to retrieve a lost treasure."

Alex picked up the paperweight again. It hovered an inch or so off the desk before he set it back down with an indelicate click. "I should think of it as what it is. A business transaction. You have been very good to me. Without your influence in my life I would likely be completely derelict. Or worse, some sort of social climber working his way through champagne and sunless tanner in South Beach."

"Dear God, what a nightmarish prospect."

"Especially as, by extension, I would be doing it with your money."

"Your point is made. I am a steadying and magnificent influence." The ghost of a smile that played across his grandfather's ancient features pleased him. "I need you to retrieve the painting for me. It took all of my strength to put my socks on and come down here today. I can hardly track across the Mediterranean to Aceena to retrieve the painting myself."

"Aceena?" Alex asked, thinking of what little he knew about the small island. With its white sand beaches and jewel-bright water, it was famous the world over.

"Yes, boy. Honestly, now I want a refund from that boarding school."

"I know where and what Aceena is, *Nonno*. But as far as I'm aware their primary attraction is alcohol and their chief import is university students on spring break."

"Yes. A hazardous side effect of beachfront property, I suppose. But also, it is where the D'Oro family has spent their banishment."

"On spring break?"

"In an estate, I'm told. Though I fear Queen Lucia's children have been on perpetual spring break ever since carving a swath of scandal through Europe. The queen lives there with her granddaughter. She was the rumored subject of the painting—" his grandfather paused "—and the last person to have it. So I've heard."

Alex wasn't a fool, and he didn't appreciate that the old man was playing him for one. Giovanni wouldn't send him off to Aceena because of half-heard rumors. And he would know full well who the subject of that painting was, had it been in his possession.

Leave it to Giovanni to have a portrait of a disgraced queen in his collection of lost treasures.

"You seem to know a great deal about the royal family," Alex said.

"I have some ties to Isolo D'Oro. I…visited for a time. There are…fond memories for me there and I carry the history with me."

"Fascinating."

"You don't have to be fascinated, Alessandro, you have to do my bidding."

Of course, if Giovanni asked, Alex had to comply. He *owed* him. Giovanni had raised Alex after the death of his parents. Had given him a job, instilled in him the work ethic that had made him so successful.

Without Giovanni, Alex was nothing.

And if his grandfather's dream was to see his Lost Mistresses reunited, then Alex would be damned if he was the weak link in the chain.

Enough suffering in his family was tied to his pig-headedness. He would not add this to the list.

"As you wish," Alex said.

"You're turning this into a clichéd movie, Alessandro."

"A quest for a hidden painting secreted away on an island by disgraced royals? I think we were already there."

CHAPTER TWO

"THERE IS A man at the door, here to see Queen Lucia."

Princess Gabriella looked up from the book she was reading and frowned. She was in the library, perched on a velvet chair that she privately thought of as a tuffet, because it was overstuffed, with little buttons spaced evenly over the cushion, and it just *looked* like the word sounded.

She hadn't expected an interruption. Most of the household staff knew to leave her be when she was in the library.

She pulled her glasses off and rubbed her eyes, untucking her legs out from underneath her bottom and stretching them out in front of her. "I see. And why exactly does this man think he can show up unannounced and gain an audience with the queen?"

She slipped her glasses back onto her face and planted her feet firmly on the ground, her hands resting on her knees as she waited for a response.

"He is Alessandro Di Sione. An American businessman. And he says he is here to see about...to see about *The Lost Love*."

Gabriella shot to her feet, all of the blood rushing to her head. She pitched sideways, then steadied herself, waiting for the room to stop spinning.

"Are you all right, ma'am?" asked the servant, Lani.

"Fine," Gabriella said, waving her hand. "*The Lost Love?* He's looking for the painting?"

"I don't know anything about a painting, Princess."

"I do," Gabriella said, wishing she had her journal on hand so she could leaf through it. "I know plenty about it. Except for whether or not it actually exists."

She had never outright asked her grandmother about it. The older woman was loving, but reserved, and the rumors about the painting were anything but. She could hardly imagine her grandmother engaging in the scandalous behavior required for *The Lost Love* to exist… and yet. And yet she had always wondered.

"Forgive me, but it seems as though knowing whether or not something exists would be the most essential piece of information to have on it."

"Not in my world."

When it came to researching genealogical mysteries, Gabriella knew that the possibility of something was extremely important. It was the starting point. Sometimes, collecting information through legend was the key to discovering whether or not something was real. And often times, confirming the existence of something was the *final* step in the process, not the first.

When it came to establishing the facts of her family's banishment from Isolo D'Oro, legend, folktales and rumor were usually the beginning of every major breakthrough. In fact, her experience with such things was leading her to odd conclusions regarding yetis and the Loch Ness monster. After all, if multiple cultures had rumors about similar beasts, it was logical to conclude that such a thing must have a grain of truth.

But until she was able to sift through the facts and fictions of her familial heritage, she would leave cryptozoology for other people.

"What should I do with our visitor, ma'am?"

Gabriella tapped her chin. She was inclined to have their visitor told that she and her grandmother were Not at Home, in the Regency England sense of the phrase. But he knew about *The Lost Love*. She was curious what exactly he knew about it. Though she didn't want to confirm the existence of it to a total stranger. Particularly when she hadn't established the existence of it in all certainty to herself.

She had to figure out what his game was. If this was just a scammer of some sort determined to make a profit off an elderly woman—and that was likely the case—then Gabriella would have to make sure he was never given entry.

"I will speak to him. There is no sense in bothering the queen. She is taking tea in the morning room and I don't wish to disturb her."

Gabriella brushed past the servant, and headed out of the library, down the richly carpeted hall, her feet sinking into the lush, burgundy pile. She realized then that going to greet a total stranger with bare feet was not the most princess-like act. She did quite well playing her part in public. A lifetime of training made a few hours of serene smiling and waving second nature. But when she was home, here in the wonderful, isolated estate in Aceena, she shut her manners, along with her designer gowns, away. Then unwound her hair from the tight coil she wore it in when she was allowing herself to be trotted out in front of the public, and truly let herself simply be *Gabriella.*

She touched her face, her glasses. She also didn't go out in public in those.

Oh, well. She didn't want to impress this stranger; she wanted to interrogate him, and then send him on his way.

She padded through the grand entryway, not bothering with straightening her hair or preening in any way at all.

He had already been admitted entry, of course. It wouldn't do to have a man like him standing outside on the step. And she could see what kind of man he was immediately as he came into her view.

He was…striking. It reminded her of an experience she'd once had in a museum. Moving through wall after wall of spectacular art before entering a small room off to the side. In it, one painting, with all of the light focused on it. It was the centerpiece. The only piece that mattered. Everything that had come before it paled in comparison.

The journey had been lovely, but this man was the destination.

He was like a van Gogh. His face a study in slashing lines and sharp angles. Sharp cheekbones, an angular jaw roughened with dark stubble. There was a soft curve to his lips that spoke of an artist with a deft hand.

Who knew that after so much hardened and fearful symmetry there needed to be something different to draw the eye. There was a slight imperfection in his features, as well, one peak of his top lip not quite rising as high as the other. It gave a human quality to Alessandro that was missing from the rest of him. Those broad shoulders, muscular chest and slim waist covered by his severely tailored suit. Long, strong legs, feet covered by handmade shoes.

Yes, everything about him was formidable perfection.

Except for that mouth. The mouth that promised potential softening. That hinted at the fact that he was a man, rather than simply a work of art.

She blinked, shaking her head. That was a lengthy flight of romantic fantasy. Even for her.

"Hello?" She took a step deeper into the entry. "Can I help you?"

His dark eyes flickered over her, his expression one of disinterest. "I wish to speak to Queen Lucia about *The Lost Love*."

"Yes. So I was told. However, I'm afraid the queen is unavailable to visitors at the moment." She resisted the urge to push her glasses up her nose, and instead crossed her arms, trying to look slightly regal, though she was wearing black leggings and an oversize sweatshirt.

"So she sent… I give up. What are you exactly? The resident disaffected teenager? Ready to head out to a mall or some such?"

Gabriella sniffed. "Actually, I am Princess Gabriella D'Oro. So when I say that my grandmother is not available to see you, I speak from a place of authority. This is my home, and I regret to inform you that we have no space for you in it."

"Strange. It seems quite spacious to me."

"Well, things are organized just so. Quite a few too many American businessmen have been by of late. We would have to store you in the attic, and you would just collect dust up there."

"Is that so?"

"I fear you would atrophy completely."

"Well, we can't have that. This is a new suit, and I don't particularly want to atrophy in it."

"Then perhaps you should be on your way."

"I came a great distance to speak to your grandmother. This may surprise you, but I did not come to Aceena to engage in frivolity. But rather to speak to her about a painting."

"Yes, so you said. I regret to inform you there is no such painting. I'm not entirely certain what you heard about it..."

"My grandfather. He is...the collector. I came to see about purchasing the painting on his behalf. I'm willing to offer a generous sum. I imagine disgraced royals might not be in a position to turn such an offer down."

"Oh, we do just fine, thank you for your concern. Should you like to make a donation to someone in actual need of your charity, I would be happy to provide you with a list."

"No, thank you. The charity was only a side effect.

I want that painting. I'm willing to pay whatever the cost might be."

Her mouth was dry. It made it difficult to speak, and yet she found she also couldn't stop the flow of words. "Well, I'm afraid to disappoint you. While we do have paintings, we do not have that painting. That painting, if you weren't aware, might not even exist."

"Oh, I'm well aware that it's what your family would like the public to think. However, I think you know more than you're letting on."

"No," she said, and this time she did push her glasses up her nose. "I'm just a teenager headed out to the mall. What could I possibly know that you," she said, sweeping her hand up and down, "in all your infinite and aged wisdom, do not?"

"The appeal of Justin Bieber?"

"I'm not entirely certain who that is."

"I'm surprised by that. Girls your age love him."

"In that case, can I offer you a hard candy? I hear men your age love those."

She was not sure how this had happened. How she had wound up standing in the hallowed entry of her family estate trading insults with a stranger.

"I'll accept the hard candy if it means you intend to give me a tour while I finish it."

"No. Sorry. You would be finishing it on the lawn."

He rubbed his hand over his chin and she shivered, an involuntary response to the soft noise made by the scrape of his hand over his whiskers. She was a sensualist. It was one of her weaknesses. She enjoyed art, and soft cushions, desserts and lush fabrics. The smell of old books and the feel of textured pages beneath her fingertips.

And she noticed fine details. Like the sound skin made when scraping over stubble.

"I'm not entirely certain this is the tactic you want to use. Because if you send me away, then I will only circumvent you. Either by contacting your grandmother directly, or by figuring out who manages the affairs of the royal family. I am certain that I can find someone who might be tempted by what I offer."

He probably wasn't wrong. If he managed to find her parents, and offer them a bit of money—or better yet, an illegal substance—for some information on an old painting, they would be more than happy to help him. Fortunately, they probably had no idea what the painting was, much less knew any more about its existence than she did.

But they were wretched. And they were greedy. So there was very little that she would put past them.

Still, she was not going to allow him to harass her grandmother. Tempting as it was to keep him here, to question him. She'd been studying her family history for as long as she'd known how to read. Rumors about this painting had played a large part in it.

Part of her desperately wanted him to stay. Another part needed him gone as quickly as possible. Because of her grandmother. And partly because of the dry mouth and sweaty palms and strange, off-kilter feeling that had arrived along with him.

Those things defeated curiosity. He had to go.

"I'll chance it. Do feel free to meander about the

grounds before you go. The gardens are beautiful. Please consider limitless viewing time on the topiaries a conciliatory gesture on my end."

The corner of his mouth worked upward. "I assure you, I have no interest in your...topiaries."

Something about the way he said it made her scalp prickle, made her skin feel hot. She didn't like it.

"Well, my topiaries are all you're going to get. Good day to you, sir."

"And good day to you," he said, inclining his head.

He sounded perfectly calm, but a dark note wound its way around his words, through his voice, and she had a feeling that somewhere within it was also woven a threat.

However, she didn't allow him to see that she had picked up on it. Instead, she turned on her heel—ignoring the slight squeak her bare skin made on the marble tile—and walked out of the entry without a backward glance, leaving him there. She fully expected a servant would show him out. Either that or she would have to have him installed in the attic. The idea of collecting a man like him and putting him in the attic like one might do to an old, rusted suit of armor amused her.

She let that little smile linger on her lips as she made her way down the hall, toward the morning room where her grandmother was having her breakfast.

"There was a man here, Gabriella. Who was he?" The queen's voice, wispy, as thin as a cobweb, greeted Gabriella as soon as she walked into the ornate room.

There was no sense asking how her grandmother

knew about the visitor. She was never ignorant about the goings-on in her own household.

"An American businessman," Gabriella said, walking deeper into the room, feeling somewhat sheepish, yet again, about her bare feet.

Her grandmother was, as ever, impeccably dressed. The older woman made no distinction between her public and private persona. As always, her crystal white hair was pulled back into a neat bun, her makeup expertly done. Her fingernails were painted the same pale coral as the skirt she was wearing, her low, sensible heels the same cream as her blouse.

"I see," the queen said, setting her teacup down on the table in front of her. "And what did he want?"

"This is not something we've ever discussed before, I know, but he was...he was inquiring about a painting. *The Lost Love*."

Her grandmother continued to sit there, poised, her hands folded in her lap. Were it not for the subtle paling of her complexion, Gabriella would have thought she had merely been commenting on the weather. There was no mistaking her grandmother's response to what she had just said.

"But of course," Gabriella continued, "I told him that it has never been confirmed that there is any such painting. I told him it was nothing more than salacious rumor. And I sent him on his way. Though he may be meandering around the gardens."

Her grandmother turned her head to the window and Gabriella did the same. Just in time to see a figure in a dark suit pass by quickly before disappearing down the path.

Something in Lucia's expression shifted. "Call him back."

"I can't. I just…I just sent him away. That would be… Well, it would seem fickle. Plus, it's rather silly."

"You must call him back, Gabriella." When Lucia used that tone there really was no point in arguing. Still, Gabriella thought she might try.

"I don't trust him. I didn't want him to upset you."

"I need to know who he is. I need to know why he is asking about the painting. It's important." There was a thread of steel woven into her voice now, a command that Gabriella could not deny.

"Of course, Grandmother. I will go after him right away."

"For heaven's sake, girl, put some shoes on."

Gabriella nodded, turning and scampering out of the room, heading down the corridor toward her bedroom. She found a pair of easy slip-on canvas shoes, then continued to head out to the front door. It was firmly closed, the visitor nowhere to be seen.

She opened the door, heading down the paved walk, toward one of the gardens. He didn't exactly seem like the kind of person who would take her up on the offer of a garden tour, but she had to make sure. He might still be here.

Her grandmother had commanded an audience with him, and she would be darned if she would disappoint the older woman.

Her grandmother meant the world to her. Her parents had preferred a life of partying to that of raising children. Her brothers were so much older than her so she could scarcely remember a time when they had lived in the same household. As soon as Gabriella had been old enough to have a say in her own situation, she had asked to go to Aceena to live with Queen Lucia. The older woman had been more of a mother to her than her own had ever been, and she could deny her nothing.

She looked around, and she didn't see him. Of course he was gone. And she hadn't gotten any of his contact information, because she hadn't wanted it. She was annoyed. At him, at herself. But mostly at him.

She walked farther down the manicured lane, turned left at the first hedge, ran squarely into a broad back covered in very high-quality black fabric. She could tell the fabric was high quality, not just because of how it looked, but because of the way it felt squished up against her face.

She stumbled backward just as he turned to face her. He was even more arresting, even more off-putting, up close. He exuded… Well, he just exuded.

"Well, I see you were making use of my offer to tour the gardens."

He straightened his tie, the action drawing her eyes to his hands. They were very large. Naturally, as he was quite a large man. So really, they were nothing quite so spectacular. They were proportional. Useful. In possession of the typical number of fingers.

"No. I was skulking. I thought I might hang around

long enough that I can try my hand at getting an audience with your grandmother later."

"That's quite sneaky."

"Sneaky is not typically a word I associate with myself, but I'll take it. Determined, I think sums it up."

"I don't see why you can't be called both."

"Whatever makes you happy. Why exactly are you looking for me?"

"It turns out…my grandmother wants to speak to you."

"Oh," he said, a slow smile spreading over his arrogant face. "I take it you're not the voice of authority when it came to your grandmother's desires, then?"

"I was trying to protect her. Surely, you can't fault me for that."

"Sure I can. I can fault you for anything I like."

She looked hard at him. It was impossible to tell if he was teasing. Impossible to tell if he had the capacity to tease or if he was deadly serious down to his bones. "Which, in a nutshell is exactly why I couldn't allow you to see her. You're a strange man. A stranger, I mean. You also don't seem very…sensitive."

"Do I not?"

She narrowed her eyes. "No."

"Well, I shall endeavor to work on that during the walk from the garden to where your grandmother is waiting for me."

Her lips twitched, but she wouldn't allow them to stretch into a smile. "If you would be so kind as to do just that, it would be greatly appreciated."

"I live to serve."

She had no doubt he did *not*.

She led the way from the palace gardens back through to the estate; as they walked through the halls she kept her eyes on his face, trying to suss out exactly what he was thinking. His expression was neutral, and he wasn't nearly as impressed as she felt like he should be. The halls of the Aceena estate were filled with beautiful, classic art. Paintings, vases, sculpture. Really, he should be quite impressed.

She supposed that was the hazard with very rich men. It was hard to show them anything they hadn't seen before.

She had grown up in this luxury and she never took any of it for granted. There was always new beauty in the world to discover. It was why she loved art. Why she loved history. There were centuries of beauty stretching back as far as humanity had been in existence. And the future stretched before them, too. Limitless. Infinite in its possibilities. There was hardly a chance to get bored with anything.

Gabriella didn't see the point in jaded cynicism, though she knew some people found it a sign of intellectual superiority.

She just found it sad.

He was probably like her parents. Sensory seekers who were never satisfied with what was around them. Things had to be grand, loud, crowded. Otherwise, they could scarcely feel, could scarcely see.

Gabriella on the other hand needed very little to be entertained. A nicely appointed room, a good book. A lovely piece of art.

She appreciated small things. Quiet things.

She felt very sorry for those who didn't.

"She's in here," Gabriella said, pausing at the doorway.

He arched his brows. "Is she? What are you waiting for? Are you going to go in and announce me?"

"Well, very likely I *should.* I'm very sorry, I know you gave your name to the staff member who greeted you, but I seem to have forgotten it."

She was lying. Alessandro was his name, she remembered. But she didn't want him to think that he was so important he had taken up any space in her brain.

"Alex," he said.

"No last name?" she pressed.

"Di Sione."

"Should that name mean anything to my grandmother?"

He shrugged. "Unless she follows gossip about American businessmen, I don't know why it would. My grandfather made quite a name for himself both in the States and abroad, and I haven't done badly myself, neither have my various and sundry brothers and sisters. But I'm not certain why our names would matter to royalty."

"What is his interest in the painting?" Gabriella asked.

A brief pause. "He is a collector."

She didn't believe him.

Gabriella let out an exasperated breath. "Be cryptic if you must. But I'm sure there's more to the story than that."

Alex chuckled. "Oh, I'm certain there is, too, but

you make a mistake if you think I know more than I'm letting on. I think you and I might occupy very similar positions in the lives of our grandparents."

"How do you mean?"

"We are subject to their dictates."

Shocked laughter threatened to bubble to the surface and she held it in check. She was *not* going to allow him to amuse her. "Well, regardless. Come with me."

She pushed the door open and stepped inside. Her grandmother was sitting in the same seat she had been in when Gabriella had left her. But she seemed different somehow. Not quite so tall. Slightly diminished.

"Grandmother, may I present Mr. Alex Di Sione. He is here to talk to you about *The Lost Love.*"

"Yes," her grandmother said, gesturing for them to come deeper into the room. She turned her laser sharp focus onto Alex. "My granddaughter tells me you're interested in the painting."

"Yes," he said, not waiting to be invited to sit. He took his position in a chair opposite her grandmother, his long legs sprawled out in front of him, his forearms resting on the arms of the chair. He looked exceedingly unconcerned with the entire situation. Almost bored. Her grandmother, on the other hand, was tense.

"What is your interest in it?" she asked.

"I am acting on behalf of my grandfather." Alex looked out one of the floor-to-ceiling windows, at the garden beyond. "He claims the painting has some sentimental value to him."

“The painting has never been confirmed to exist,” Queen Lucia said.

“I’m well aware. But my grandfather seems to be very confident in its existence. In fact, he claims he once owned it.” His dark focus zeroed in on the queen. “He would like very much to have it back now.”

Silence settled between them. Thick and telling. A fourth presence in the room. Gabriella noticed her grandmother studying Alex’s face. She looked… She looked stricken. As though she was seeing a ghost.

“Your grandfather, you say?” she asked.

“Yes. He is getting on in years and with age has come sentimentality, I’m afraid. He is willing to pay a great deal for this painting.”

“I’m afraid I can’t help you with that,” the queen said.

“And why is that?” he asked, a dangerous note in his voice.

“I don’t have it. I haven’t possessed it for…years.”

“But the painting exists?” Gabriella asked, her heart thundering in her ears.

This was… Under any other circumstances, this would have been incredibly exciting. But Alex Di Sione was here and that just made it feel fraught.

“Yes,” her grandmother said, her voice thinner, more fragile all of a sudden. “It is very real.”

“Why have you never mentioned that before?”

“Because some things are best left buried in the past. Where they can no longer hurt you,” the queen said.

“Do you have any idea where the painting might be

now?" Alex asked, obviously unconcerned with her grandmother's pain.

"Yes, I know exactly where it is. Unfortunately, it's on Isolo D'Oro. One of the many reasons I have never been able to reclaim it."

"Where on the island is it?" he asked, his tone uncompromising.

"You wait outside for a moment, young man," the queen said, her tone regal, leaving no doubt at all that she had ruled a nation for a great many years and expected her each command to be obeyed without question.

And Alex didn't question it. Strange, since she imagined he wasn't a man who bowed to many. But at her grandmother's request, he stood, brushing the creases from his dress pants and nodded his head before he made his way out the door.

"You must go with him to find the painting," her grandmother said the moment he was out of earshot.

"Why?" Gabriella asked, her heart pounding in her ears.

"I… I should like to see it again. One last time. And because…because just in case, I shouldn't like for this man to be in possession of it if he is a fraud."

"I don't understand," Gabriella said, trying to process all of the information being given to her. "If he's a fraud in *what* way?"

"It isn't important."

"I think it must be quite important. We've never discussed the painting, but I've long suspected that it was real. I know…I know it was controversial. I know that it concerns you."

"Yes," her grandmother said. "At the time it was quite controversial. Evidence that…that the princess had a lover."

Her grandmother had been the princess then. Young. Unmarried. And it had been a very different time.

It was difficult to imagine her grandmother taking a lover. Difficult to imagine her doing anything quite so passionate or impetuous. She was the incomparable matriarch of the family. The figurehead so established, so steady, she might very well already be carved of marble, as she would now no doubt be in the future.

But if the painting existed, then she was the subject. And if that were the case, then of course it had been commissioned by a lover.

"I see," Gabriella said. "And…*did* you?"

Her grandmother let out a long, slow breath, raising her eyes to meet hers. In them, Gabriella could see so much. A wealth of sadness. Deep heartbreak.

Things Gabriella had read about, but never experienced.

"It is very easy when you are young, Gabriella, to lead with your heart instead of your head. You have seen this, time and again, with your parents. And they no longer carry youth as an excuse. This is why I have always told you that you must be in possession of your wits. It does not do well for a woman to lose her mind over passion. It doesn't end well. Not for us. Men can carry on as they see fit, but it isn't like that for women."

Gabriella nodded slowly. "Yes, I know." She thought

of her brothers, who most certainly carried on exactly as they pleased. Of her father, who seemed to escape the most scathing comments. The worst of it was always reserved for her mother. She was a renowned trollop whose every choice, from her wardrobe to which man she chose to make conversation with at a social event, was analyzed, was taken as evidence of her poor character.

Gabriella knew this was true. It was just one of the many reasons that she had chosen to embrace her more bookish nature and keep herself separate from all of that carrying-on.

"Our hearts are not proper guides," her grandmother continued. "They are fickle, and they are easily led. Mine certainly was. But I learned from my mistakes."

"Of course," Gabriella agreed, because she didn't know what else to say.

"Go with him," Queen Lucia said, her tone stronger now. Decisive. "Fetch the painting. But remember this conversation. Remember what I have told you."

"I don't think there's any danger of my heart getting involved on a quest of this nature."

"He is a handsome man, Gabriella."

Gabriella laughed. "He's a stranger! And old enough to be... Not my father, *certainly* not. But perhaps a young uncle."

The queen shook her head. "Men like that have their ways."

"And I have my way of scaring them off. Please, tell me when a man last danced with me more than once at a social function?"

"If you didn't speak so much of books..."

"And weevils." She had talked incessantly about weevils and the havoc they played in early English kitchens to her last dance partner. Because they had been the subject of the last book she'd read and she hadn't been able to think of anything else.

"Certainly don't speak of that."

"Suffice it to say I don't think you have to worry about me tumbling into a romance. The only problem is... Why would he take me with him? Now that he knows the painting exists, and that it is on Isolo D'Oro, he'll no doubt have an easy enough time figuring out *where* it is. And I'm sure he'll have no trouble finding someone to impart what information they might have about it, for the right price."

"No," her grandmother said, "he won't."

"Why is that?"

"Because. Because *you* have the key. You're the only one who has the key."

Gabriella frowned. "I don't have a key."

"Yes, you do. The painting is hidden away in one of the old country estates that used to belong to the royal family. It is in a secret room, behind a false wall, and no one would have found it. So long as the building stands, and I have never heard rumors to the contrary, the painting would have remained there."

"And the key?"

Her grandmother reached out, her shaking hands touching the necklace that Gabriella wore. "Close to your heart. Always."

Gabriella looked down at the simple flower pendant that hung from the gold chain she wore around her neck. “My necklace?”

It had been a gift to her when she was a baby. A piece of the family’s crown jewels that her mother had considered beneath her. So simple, but lovely, a piece of art to Gabriella’s mind.

“Yes, your necklace. Did you ever wonder why the bottom of it had such an odd shape? Once you get into this room, you fit this into a slot on the picture frame on the back wall. It swings open and, behind it, you will find *The Lost Love*.”

CHAPTER THREE

TRULY, HIS GRANDFATHER had a lot to answer for. Alex was not the kind of man accustomed to doing the bidding of anyone but himself. And yet, here he was, cooling his heels in the antechamber of a second-rate country estate inhabited by disgraced royals.

If he were being perfectly honest—and he always was—one royal in particular who looked more like a small, indignant owl than she did a princess.

With her thick framed glasses and rather spiky demeanor it did not seem to him that Princess Gabriella was suited to much in the way of royal functions. Not that he was a very good barometer of exceptional social behavior.

Alex was many things, *acceptable* was the least among them.

Normally, he would not have excused himself from the room quite so quickly. Normally, he would have sat there and demanded that all the information be disseminated in his presence. Certainly, Queen Lucia was a queen. But in his estimation it was difficult to be at one's full strength when one did not have a country to rule. In truth, the D'Oro family had not inhabited a throne in any real sense in more years than Princess Gabriella had been alive.

So while the family certainly still had money, and a modicum of power, while they retained their titles, he did not imagine he would bring the wrath of an army down on his head for refusing a direct order.

However, he had sensed then that it was an opportune moment to test the theory of catching more flies with honey than vinegar.

He did so hate having to employ charm.

He had better end up in possession of the painting. And it had better truly be his grandfather's dying wish. Otherwise, he would be perturbed.

The door behind him clicked shut and he turned just in time to see Princess Gabriella, in her fitted sweatshirt and tight black leggings, headed toward him. She was holding her hands up beneath her breasts like a small, frightened animal, her eyes large behind her glasses.

That was what had put him in the mind of her being an owl earlier. He did not feel the need to revise that opinion. She was fascinating much in the way a small creature might be.

He felt compelled to watch her every movement, her every pause. As he would any foreign entity. So, there was nothing truly remarkable about it.

"Well, my princess," he said. "What have you learned?"

"I know where the painting is," she said, tucking a silken strand of dark hair behind her ear before returning her hands back to their previous, nervous position.

"Excellent. Draw me a map on a napkin and I'll be on my way."

"Oh. There will be no direction giving. No napkin drawing."

"Is that so?"

She tossed her hair and for a moment he saw a glimmer of royalty beneath her rather dowdy exterior. And that was all the more fascinating. "No. I'm not giving you directions, because *I* have the directions. You are taking me with you."

He laughed at the imperious, ridiculous demand. "I most certainly am not."

She crossed her arms, the sweater bunching beneath them. "Yes, you are. You don't know how to get there."

"Gabriella, I am an expert at getting the information I want. Be it with money or seduction, it makes no difference to me, but I will certainly get what I need."

Her cheeks turned a rather fetching shade of pink. He imagined it was the mention of seduction, not bribery, that did it.

"But *I* have the key," she insisted. "Or rather, I know where it is. And trust me when I tell you it is not something you'll be able to acquire on your own."

"A key?" He didn't believe her.

"And the…the instructions on how to use it."

He studied her hard. She was a bookish creature. Not terribly beautiful, in his estimation. Not terribly brave, either. Intensely clever, though. Still, the lack of bravery made it unlikely that she was lying to him. The cleverness, on the other hand, was a very large question mark.

It made her unpredictable.

This was why he preferred women who were not so clever.

Life was complicated enough. When it came to interactions with the female sex he rather liked it simple, physical and brief.

He had a feeling his association with Gabriella would be none of those things and that only set his teeth on edge all the more.

"I do not believe that you have the key, or rather, have access to it that I cannot gain."

"Okay, then. Enjoy the journey to Isolo D'Oro without me. I'm sure when you get there and find that you hold nothing in your hand but your own—"

"Well, now, there's no need to get crass."

She blinked. "I wasn't going to be crass. I was going to say you hold nothing in your hand but your own arrogance."

He chuckled. "Well, I was imagining you saying something completely different."

"What can I have possibly—?" She blinked again. "Oh."

He arched a brow. "Indeed."

She gritted her teeth, her expression growing more fierce. "Crassness and all other manner of innuendo aside, you are not gaining access to the painting without me."

"Right. So, you know where it is, and you clearly possess the key. Why not go without me?"

"Well, it isn't that simple. I am a member of the D'Oro family. And while technically I can return to the island because I am only of the bloodline, and I never ruled, gaining access could still be a problem."

"I see. So, how do we play this? Wealthy American businessman on a vacation takes a beautiful…" He paused for a moment, allowing his eyes to sweep over her, not hiding how underwhelmed he was by the sight. "A beautiful princess as his lover?"

"Absolutely not!" She turned a very intense shade of pink, and he found himself captivated by the slow bleed of color beneath her skin.

"You have a better suggestion?"

"I want to prevent scandal. I want to bring the painting back here with as little fanfare as possible. I don't want you making a big production of things."

"And I assure you I will not. This is for a private collection and has nothing to do with causing embarrassment to the royal family."

She worried her lip between her teeth. "I don't trust you."

"Excellent. I wouldn't trust me, either."

"Excellent. No trust." Her cheeks were getting redder. This time, he figured it was from frustration. "I want to go with you. But I don't want to cause a scene. I can't cause a scene. You have no doubt seen the kind of scandal my parents create in the headlines with their drug use, affairs, separations, reconciliations… The press would love to smell blood in the water around me and I just can't chance it."

An evil thought occurred to him and it made him smile. "Well, if you don't wish to go as my lover—"

"I don't!"

"Then I'm afraid you'll have to come as my assistant."

"No one will believe that I'm your assistant. I'm a princess." She lifted her little nose in the air, dark hair cascading over her back like spilled ink. Now she did indeed look every inch insulted royalty.

"What do you typically look like when you go out and about? I imagine it isn't like this," he said, indicating her rather drab trappings.

"I don't go out frequently. But when I do I have a stylist."

"Your glasses?"

"I normally wear contacts."

He nodded slowly. "Princess Gabriella D'Oro. I *have* seen pictures of you—it's only that I would never have recognized you in your current state. The difference is remarkable."

He had an immediate picture in his mind of a glossier, more tamed version of the woman in front of him. Sleek and, actually, quite beautiful. Though not remotely as interesting as the version of Gabriella that stood before him.

She waved a hand. "Between professionally fitted dresses, undergarments to hold in all undesirable lumps and bumps, makeup to cover every flaw, false eyelashes, red lips… I'm scarcely the same person."

"A good thing for our current situation." He regarded her for a longer period of time. "Yes, that will do nicely. You will come as my assistant. With your hair just like this. With your glasses. And with some horrible pantsuit. No one will ever believe you are Princess Gabriella. No one will look twice at you. Certainly not close enough to identify you. That eases any and all problems we might have with the press, with the local government and with scandal."

He could see that she was fuming, *radiating* with indignity. He quite liked it. He didn't have a lot of time. He certainly didn't have *extra* time to stand around negotiating about keys and directions with a silly girl.

So she would come. It was no difference to him either way.

"That is a ridiculous idea," she said. "Anyway, I've never traveled. I mainly stay here in the estate."

"Curled up on a cushion reading a book?"

She blinked. "What else would one do on a cushion?"

"Oh, I can think of several things."

"Drinking tea?"

"No. Not drinking tea."

Her expression was a study in confusion. It was almost cute. Except that he had no interest in bookish virgins.

She was…naive. Young. For a moment he was concerned about how young. "How old are you?"

She sniffed. "I'm twenty-three. You can stop looking at me like I'm some sort of schoolgirl."

"*Cara mia*, you are a schoolgirl to me."

"How old are *you*?"

"That is none of your business."

"Am I to respect my elders?"

He laughed, he couldn't help it. Rare was the person who poked back at him. He rather enjoyed having fun at other people's expense, but they didn't dare have it at his.

His secret was that he found it rather entertaining

just how afraid everyone seemed to be in his presence. His formidable reputation afforded him a great deal of enjoyment. Though the fact that he took pleasure in making people quake in his presence was likely why he had so few friends. Not that he minded.

He had sycophants, he had business associates and he had mistresses. He had no room in his life for anything else. Nor had he the desire for them.

Unfortunately, he also had family, and with them came obligations. Family was, after all, how he found himself here now.

"Then it is decided. You will be my personal assistant, a college student, doing a work experience program. Traveling with me to Isolo D'Oro to take in some of the local culture and scenery while I negotiate a business deal."

"I'm supposed to be your…intern?" She was positively incandescent with irritation now.

"Yes. Of course, Gabriella is a little bit posh for that. How about Gabby? It has a very nice ring to it. Don't you think, *Gabby*?"

"I hate being called Gabby."

"But I'll wager you hate scandal even more. So, Gabby my assistant you will be, and we will not create any of it."

She frowned, her dark brows lowering, disappearing behind the thick frame of her glasses. "If you're going to be this exasperating for the entire journey I can see it's going to be a problem."

"I don't plan on being this exasperating for the entire journey." She breathed out a sigh of relief. "I plan on being at least twice as exasperating."

Her eyes flew wide. "And why is that?"

"Oftentimes I find life short on entertainment. I do my best to make my own fun."

"Yes, well, I live in an estate with an old woman in her nineties. I make a lot of my own fun, too. But typically that involves complicated genealogy projects and a little bit of tatting."

"Tatting?"

"You can never have too many doilies. Not in a house this size."

He arched a brow, studying her face to see if she was being sincere. He couldn't get a read on her. "I will have to take your word for that."

"Don't you have doilies?"

He lifted his shoulder. "I might in one of my residences. I can't say that I ever noticed."

"I could make you some. No one should have a doily deficiency."

"God forbid." He turned and began to walk away from her. "Aren't you going to show me to my room?"

"Excuse me?" she asked.

"Aren't you going to show me to my room?" he repeated. "We will leave early tomorrow morning for Isolo D'Oro. I don't see any point in my staying elsewhere. You have a great many rooms in the estate. And they are replete with doilies, I hear. Which means you should be able to accommodate me."

He turned his most charming and feral smile in her

direction. Usually women shrank back from them. Or swooned.

She did neither.

"I did not invite you to stay. And it's particularly impolite of you to invite yourself."

"It wasn't particularly hospitable of *you* to not invite me. I will put aside my pique for the sake of convenience, and a more companionable journey tomorrow. Now," he said, his tone uncompromising. He excelled at being uncompromising. "Be a good girl and show me to my room."

CHAPTER FOUR

"WHAT IS THIS?"

Gabriella came out of the bedroom positioned toward the back of his private jet. She was wearing her glasses, as instructed, her dark hair pulled back into a ponytail. She was also newly dressed in the outfit he had gone to great lengths to procure for her before his plane had departed this morning for Isolo D'Oro. Well, one of the palace servants had gone to great lengths to procure it. He had taken a rather leisurely breakfast during which he had checked his stocks and made sure that things were running smoothly back at his office in Manhattan.

"Your costume, Gabby," he said.

Had she been an owl he was certain that at the moment her feathers would have been ruffled. "It isn't very flattering."

"Well, neither was the sweatshirt you were wearing when we met yesterday. But that did not seem to stop you from wearing it."

"I was having a day at home. I had been sitting in the library reading."

"Naturally."

She frowned. "What does that mean?"

"You look like the type. That's all."

She shifted slightly, her frown deepening. "Yes, I suppose so. But I'm not entirely lacking in vanity. This…" She indicated the black dress pants, tapered closely to her skin—much more closely than he had anticipated—and the white blouse she was wearing, complete with a large pin that should have looked more at home on her grandmother than on her, but managed to look quite stylish. "This is not the kind of thing I'm used to wearing in public."

She didn't look like a princess—that much was true. But the outfit was not actually unflattering. The outfit was very nearly fashionable, albeit in a much lower-rent way than she was no doubt used to looking.

"What exactly is the problem with it?"

"The pants are very tight."

"Their most redeeming feature in my opinion."

He was rewarded with another of her blushes. "I do not like to draw attention to my body."

"Believe me when I tell you this, Gabriella. You do not have to do anything to draw attention to your body. The very fact that it exists does draw attention to it." He found it was true even as he spoke the words. He had not readily noticed her charms upon his arrival at the estate yesterday, but she was certainly not lacking in them. Her figure was not what was considered attractive these days. There was no careful definition of muscles earned through long hours in a gym. No gap between her thighs.

She was lush. Soft. Average-size breasts that were remarkable if only because breasts always were, a slender waist and generously rounded hips. Hips that were currently being flaunted by the pants she was complaining about.

"Oh. Well. That is… Was that a compliment?"

"Yes. It was a good compliment."

"Sorry. I'm not used to receiving compliments from men."

He found that hard to believe. She was a princess. Moreover, she wasn't unattractive. Usually one or the other was enough. "Do you ever leave the estate?"

"In truth, not that often."

"That must be your problem. Otherwise, I imagine you would be inundated with compliments. Sincere and otherwise."

"Why is that?"

"Because. You have quite a few things men would find desirable."

"Money."

"That is certainly one of the things. Though right now you could easily pass for a personal assistant. Which is exactly what we are going for." He took a seat in one of the plush armchairs and picked up the mug of coffee he had poured himself earlier.

"What are the other things?"

"Your body. And its various charms. I thought I made that clear."

She frowned. He expected her to…well, to get angry. Or shrink up against the wall like all bookish virgins should do. Instead, she walked through the plane and took the seat opposite from him, crossing her legs at the ankles and folding her hands in her lap. "You're very blunt."

"Yes. I find it frightens people. Which I very much enjoy."

"I'm not certain if I'm blunt in quite the same way you are. But I do tend to say whatever pops into my mind. Often it's about something unrelated to the situation. That also seems to frighten people. Men specifically."

"The reason you don't receive many compliments?"

"My mother always told me to keep conversation to the topic of the weather. But we live on an island. Unless a hurricane or tsunami is threatening, the weather isn't all that interesting."

"That's the point. A great many men prefer their women to be dull on the inside and shiny on the outside."

"You among them?"

He chuckled. "Oh, I am *chief* among them."

She tilted her head to the side, a rather bemused and curious expression on her face. "Why is that?"

"Why is what, *cara mia*?"

"Why do so many men prefer their women to be quite the opposite of what one should prefer in a person?"

"Because. Those sorts of men, myself included, don't want women for sparkling conversation. They want them for one thing, and one thing only."

She sighed, a rather heavy, irritated sound. "I imagine you mean sex."

He was momentarily surprised by her directness. Not that directness shocked him in any manner; it was simply that this kind of directness coming from *her* was shocking.

"Yes," he said, not seeing why he shouldn't be equally direct in return.

"Predictable. I suppose that's why my mother is able to skip through life behaving so simply. She's a prime example of what you're talking about. Someone who is all sparkle and shine. My father no longer even possesses any shine. But I imagine in his case it's the promise of money and an eventual payoff that bring women into his bed."

"That sounds quite familiar to me."

She studied him, a confused expression crossing her face. "But—and I'm speaking in a continued metaphor—you seem to be *quite* shiny."

He laughed. No one had ever characterized him as shiny before. "I wasn't thinking of myself. It's true, I have my own set of charms that bring females into my bed. Money. Looks, so they tell me. But in this case I was thinking of my parents."

"Oh?"

"Yes. It sounds very much like they would have been friends with yours."

"Do your parents enjoy drugs, wild affairs and questionable fashion sense?"

He laughed, but this time the sound was bitter. "They liked nothing more. In fact, they loved it so much it killed them."

She seemed to shrink in her seat, the regret on her

face pronounced. "Oh. I'm sorry. I should not have made light of it. Not without knowing your background."

He picked up his clear mug of coffee and turned it until the light coming from outside the plane window caught hold of the amber liquid, setting it ablaze. "One *must* make light of these things. Otherwise, it's all darkness, isn't it?"

"Some things are only dark, I fear."

He shrugged, taking another drink. "They don't have to be."

"How did your parents die?"

The question struck him. She genuinely didn't know. But then, it stood to reason. She'd had no idea who he was when they had first met. Rare was the person who didn't know his entire family history before introducing themselves to him. She was an odd creature. And her cleverness was *still* off-putting. But he found small pieces of her to be a breath of fresh air he hadn't realized he'd been craving.

"They died in a car accident," he said. "They were having one of their legendary fights. Fueled by alcohol, drugs and a sexual affair. Basically, all of their favorite things combined into one great fiery ball of doom."

"Oh. That's awful."

"Yes. I suppose it is. But I was very young. And not much a part of their lives." He did his best to keep the memories of that night from crowding in. Snowy. The roads filled with ice. His parents shrieking obscenities. And a small boy standing out in the cold, looking lost and lonely. "I find them a tragedy. A cautionary tale. I might be a bit jaded, but I'm not a total libertine. I suppose I have their tragedy to thank for that."

She nodded, as though she completely understood what he was talking about. He had no doubt she had little experience of libertines outside the pages of a book.

"If it weren't for my parents," she said, her words coming slowly, "who knows how I would be? It is their example that has kept me so firmly planted in the estate in Aceena. It's their example that has caused me to crave a quieter existence."

That surprised him. It seemed she *did* understand. At least a little bit better than he had guessed she might. A little bit better than most.

All of his siblings had started life with the same parents he had, and yet he had been the only one affected in quite this way.

His twin brothers were hellions. They were playboys who lived their lives entirely as they saw fit. At least, they *had* been before their respective *true loves* had come into their lives.

But always, they had lived with much more passion than Alex ever had. Even now that they had settled down, they continued to live with more passion and emotion than Alex would ever consider.

"Everything makes much more sense if you see life as a business," he said, speaking the thought before he had decided he would.

"Do you think so?"

He nodded. "Yes. Business is sensible. Everyone is in it to make money. That's the bottom line. Because of that, everyone's motives are transparent from the beginning. They're going to serve themselves. Sometimes favors are traded. Contracts are drawn up, terms are met."

"A bit more clear-cut than people," she said.

"I've always found it slightly strange that divorce is much easier than breaking a business contract. If people took marriage as seriously as they took business deals, the world would be a different place." He leaned back in his chair. "Of course, you could go about metaphorically hopping into bed with other partners after taking on exclusive deals with another. But you would quickly lose your credibility, and your business with it. It wouldn't serve your bottom line. Personal relationships are much more murky. There is no common bottom line. I find that disturbing."

"I see what you're saying," she said. "I hadn't thought about it that way. But then, I suppose it's because I don't have a head for business."

"What is it you have a head for, Gabby?"

She bristled at the nickname. "Books, I suppose."

"What sorts of books?"

"All sorts."

His eyes narrowed. "You said you liked genealogy."

"Yes. I do. I'm very interested in my family history. I find it completely fascinating. I believe that history contains truths. I mean, history goes beyond what's been published in the media. What the press reports… that isn't real history."

"I suppose the granddaughter of some of the world's most infamous disgraced royals would feel that way."

She lifted her shoulder, an unconscious gesture

she seemed to do a lot. She had a very delicate frame; whether in glasses or ill-fitting clothing, that couldn't be denied. She was like a strange, old-fashioned doll.

He was rather disturbed by the part of him that felt compelled to lean in and pull her from the shelf, so to speak.

"I suppose I would," she said. "But that isn't why I'm doing this. I quite like the idea of uncovering the truth, in an unbiased fashion."

"And so you study your family history."

"Yes."

Her eyes had grown brighter when the subject was introduced. Strangely, he found he quite liked it. It was very interesting to make conversation with a woman about something other than shallow topics. And in this instance, it had been quite easy. Was she truly so different?

It made him wonder if the women he conversed with were actually as shallow as he imagined or if they thought *him* to be shallow. Strange that it should matter to him at all. It shouldn't. Not when he purposefully kept those interactions as meaningless as possible.

He kept a wall between himself and others, using all manner of methods, and limited conversation with his lovers was one of those methods.

It didn't matter what he thought of them. It didn't matter what they thought of him. It only mattered how it felt when they were in bed.

"You will find this trip back to your homeland fascinating, then."

He wanted to try out a bit more of that excitement.

He wondered what it must be like, to possess that level of enthusiasm. God knew he no longer had the ability. He had seen what happened with passion. Had seen it firsthand when his parents were killed, lost forever in a storm of twisted steel and broken glass. He had no desire to be a part of anything like that. He led with his mind. He had relationships that were mutually beneficial for both parties involved.

They never ended in screams and accusations of infidelity. No. He always gave his women a gift, made sure he complimented their beauty, lied about how diverting he found their company and promised to cherish their time together always and to remember them fondly.

He never did.

The moment they walked out of his bedroom he forgot their names. He simply didn't possess the capacity to care about people with any real depth. At least, people outside of his family.

He couldn't see the value in it. He could only see the cost.

"I expect it will be wonderful. My grandmother has told me stories about the old family estates. About the palaces. But I've never been to see them myself. All I've ever seen are old, faded pictures."

"Why exactly was the royal family expelled from the country?"

"Oh, there are a great many rumors of unfair taxation. Of my great-grandfather being a tyrant. Greedy. But I'm not entirely convinced. And certainly, that isn't my grandmother's take on the situation. Regardless, there was an uprising and the family had to escape in the dead of night. They're lucky to have escaped with their lives. Most royal families don't make out quite so well during violent depositions."

"You speak the truth there."

"I think I'll be the first in my family to set foot on Isolo D'Oro since then. It's probably a good thing that I'll be incognito."

"Probably."

She smiled, her whole face brightening. It was like watching light shift over the ocean. The color moving from slate gray to a brilliant blue. "This is all a bit like a good adventure story, don't you think?"

It reminded him of something his grandfather had said. About the whole thing being like a boy's adventure. Why were people eternally attempting to excite him about something that felt like little more than a menial task?

"I consider it an errand," he said, lifting his glass to his lips again. "One that I intend to do and do well, because as I said, I believe in business. In fairness. I owe my grandfather and I am determined to repay him. But that's it."

His dry response doused her smile and he cursed himself. "Well, I think anything can be considered an errand with the incorrect mind-set. And anything can be a game if you purpose for it to be."

"All I need is a spoonful of sugar?"

She smiled. "It couldn't hurt."

"No, I suppose it couldn't." The plane began to descend, and Alex could see the scenery below growing larger. Could begin to make out the whitecaps of the waves on the bright water. “You had better buckle yourself, Princess. We are about to arrive in Isolo D’Oro. And that is the last time you will be called *Princess* for the foreseeable future.”

CHAPTER FIVE

GABRIELLA WAS STUNNED by the view spread before her. Her grandmother had told her how beautiful her homeland was, but she hadn't been prepared for the true splendor of it.

The city that she and Alex were staying in was filled with ornate, old-world architecture, the Mediterranean Sea spread out before it like a gem. It was a glorious mixture of old and new. High-rises being built in a new section of the city, dedicated to bringing much needed commerce to the nation. While the old historic districts remained unchanged.

She wanted to go out and explore. She did *not* want to cool her heels in the grand hotel suite that Alex had installed them in. But Alex had insisted that he had some work to do, and it would not do to have her wandering around the country by herself.

She supposed that she could defy him on the matter, but she honestly had such limited travel experience that she didn't feel terribly inclined to do that. She was much more likely to stick close to the large American businessman acting as her escort, as she had a feeling he would be a little bit more accomplished at guarding her physical safety than she would.

Not that anything about Isolo D'Oro seemed menacing, but stories of how her family had escaped under threat echoed in her mind. It wasn't something she could simply forget.

"How are your impressions so far?"

Alex chose that moment to come out of his bedroom. He had discarded his suit jacket, his white shirt unbuttoned at the collar, revealing a wedge of tan skin covered with just the right amount of dark chest hair.

She questioned that thought the moment it entered her mind. What on earth was the appropriate amount of chest hair, and how was she so certain that he was in possession of it? It wasn't as though she was an expert on men's chests or the quantity of hair on them.

How strange that she was putting so much thought into his.

"It's lovely," she said, turning her focus back to the view, and resolutely away from his chest.

"I'm glad you think so."

She studied him closely. "Are you?"

He smiled and the impact of it felt like a punch in the chest. He was an irritatingly large presence. His every movement set the hairs on her arms on end, his shifting expressions creating a seismic reaction in her internal organs.

"No," he said. "I don't actually care what you think. It just seemed a polite thing to say."

She looked at him, unable to get a genuine read

on him. “I can’t decide whether or not I’m amused by you,” she said.

“I believe the general consensus of me is that I’m *horrifying*.”

“Hmm. Really?”

“My reputation precedes me in all corners of the earth. I’m known to be quite hard. Demanding. A perfectionist in areas of business. Sometimes scarcely human. Some say that if you cut me, I would, in fact, not bleed.”

“Well, that is ridiculous. Because everybody bleeds,” she said.

“For such a clever creature, you are alarmingly literal.”

“It is ridiculous,” she insisted. “All of it. Obviously you’re human.”

His smile only grew broader. “*Is* it obvious? I feel it isn’t to many. But then, I find that amusing and don’t do much to dispel the idea that I might be some kind of monster.”

“Why?”

He walked across the small living area, heading back toward the bedroom he had just come out of and pushing the door open. “Coming?” he asked.

Her heart slammed against her rib cage. “What?”

“You asked a question. I thought you might want to hear the answer. But I have to go into my room to get my jacket and retrieve my tie.”

She scrambled after him, feeling a little bit silly that she had somehow read something *else* into those words. Of course he wasn’t asking her to come into the bedroom for…well, anything that might be done in the bedroom.

She wasn't the kind of woman who invited seduction. And she was genuinely fine with that. Someday, she would find a man. A suitable man who would make a suitable match. Possibly a minor role. Or someone who moved in high European society but who also liked books and dusty libraries. Yes, that. Most likely. Definitely not an American businessman who took joy in tormenting others with his dry sense of humor and seemed to regard her love of reading and research with the kind of curiosity one usually reserved for a bug under a microscope.

"You want to know why I enjoy keeping others at a distance?"

"I am curious, I admit," she said.

She was also surprised that he was even pretending he was going to give her an answer. After all, if he truly enjoyed keeping people at a distance, why would he disclose any information that might bring the two of them closer together? It didn't make sense.

"I like the freedom it affords me," he said. He opened up the closet and pulled out a jacket and a tie. Both black, exactly like the ones he'd worn earlier. Though she had a feeling they were a different set than before. "When people fear you they tend to defer to you. That ensures I get my way most of the time."

"What are they afraid you'll do?"

"I don't know." He began to button his shirt collar. "That's the most amusing part. For all the rumors of my misdeeds, I have yet to actually throw anyone in a dungeon. Neither have I ever sucked anyone's blood. However, my legend looms large, and who am I to argue with that?"

"I don't think I have a legend. Well, obviously I don't, as you had never heard of me when you arrived at the estate."

He lifted a shoulder as he looped the tie around his neck. "But then, you had never heard of me, either, *cara*."

"True enough. But I'm rather cloistered there at the estate. There are a great many things I haven't heard of."

He arched a dark brow. "Does your grandmother not have Wi-Fi?"

"Yes, we have the internet. It's just that I don't often make use of it."

"And why is that?"

"It's very disconcerting to know you could log into a news website at any time and your family is the headline. I just..." Her stomach twisted just thinking about it. "I prefer to avoid it. My brothers... Well, they're as rich as you are. Just as ruthless. Libertines, as you put it earlier. My parents are worse. At least my brothers have some good qualities to redeem them. They are amusing. When they want to be. And they're quite nice actually. To me. Their ex-mistresses would tell you a different story. But even if they've earned it...even if parts of it are true...I don't really enjoy seeing what the media has to say about my family."

"No," he said, his voice softer all of a sudden. "You prefer to gather facts."

"Yes. Exactly that."

"You like to control the story."

She shook her head. "No, it isn't about me controlling a story. I want to know the truth."

"That's a lie, Gabby. You like to control the story. You like to hear it first. You like to decide what is done with it. You want to make sure that you are able to collect the information at the speed in which you can process it. You like to ensure that you are the one who gets to form the first opinion. There isn't anything wrong with it. But it is the truth."

She felt as though he'd run her through with a scabbard. It hurt terribly and made her feel exposed. As though he'd seen down deep into parts of her she'd never even examined before.

And the only reason it felt that way was because... it was true.

"Why is it you seem to think you know me so well?" she asked.

His dark eyes leveled with hers. "I recognized something of myself in you. On that same topic, I'm never entirely certain whether or not you amuse me."

She looked down, clasping her hands together and picking at her thumbnail. "Not very many people find me amusing. I think they find me boring."

"Now that, I can't imagine. You are the farthest thing from boring. In fact, I find that to be one of your foremost negative qualities."

She frowned. "Why would being entertaining be a negative quality?"

"Because I *like* boring women. Boring women are

easy to sleep with and forget about. Boring women are the best kind."

A rash of heat broke out over her skin, color flooding her face. "I'm not going to sleep with you so my…. *interestingness* shouldn't be a problem for you."

He chuckled. "I wasn't making an offer."

Shame washed over her. Of course he wasn't. Of course he hadn't meant that. But she was still talking and she couldn't stop herself. "When I do make room in my life for that sort of relationship, I will most definitely be pursuing a man closer to my own age who has interests in common with my own."

"Oh, right. I forgot. We have quite the generational gap between us."

"It's prohibitive. We won't even like the same music."

He chuckled softly. "But you don't like popular music. You like classical music."

This statement infuriated her, because it was true, too. Just like the last one. Was she somehow telegraphing her private thoughts via her eyeballs?

"And what sort of music do you like?" she asked.

"Classic rock." He smiled. "You're right, it isn't to be. We're too different."

"Ah, well, just allow me to get the broom and dustpan so I can sweep up the pieces of my broken heart."

"I would, but we haven't the time for such carrying-on. We have a meeting."

She blinked rapidly. "We do?"

"Yes. We have a meeting with the prime minister of Isolo D'Oro."

"But… When?"

He raised his hand and looked down at his wrist, at the watch he wore that no doubt cost more than some people's yearly salary. "In about ten minutes."

She took in his perfectly pressed appearance. The sharp white shirt, and the rest, all an inky black to match his hair and eyes. He was like a dark angel come to life in Armani. And she was…well, she was wearing polyester pants.

"Wait a second! That isn't fair. You had a chance to change your clothes. I'm still wearing the same thing that I was wearing on the plane."

"Which is perfect. Because you are my assistant, not a lover. Not a princess." He reached back into the closet and pulled out a garment bag. "So, in the next ten minutes, I would like you to make sure that you put this out for the hotel staff. The jacket I was wearing earlier. It needs to be cleaned."

She sputtered. "I'm going to meet the prime minister of Isolo D'Oro in these ridiculous skinny…pants… whatever they are. And now I have to do your menial chores?"

"Well, Gabby, had we decided to go with the story that you were my current mistress I would have draped you in silks. As it is, I'm going to have to drape you in my dry cleaning."

She sniffed. "You don't have to enjoy this so much."

He chuckled, a darkly amused sound. "Oh, yes, I absolutely do have to enjoy this. As I told you before, I'm accustomed to making my own fun. And I'm finding this quite unexpectedly fun."

CHAPTER SIX

THE TROUBLE WITH meeting politicians was that they always came with an unreasonable amount of security detail and other various hangers-on. Of course, there were a few paparazzi, as well. But Alex knew that the prime minister was the quickest way to gaining access to the various historic sites they would *need* access to in order to find *The Lost Love.*

Most of the dining room had been cleared in preparation for his arrival, and it was almost entirely empty except for the three of them, seated at a table in the far corner.

When the man had finally arrived at the hotel restaurant a good fifteen minutes after he had said he would, he had spent an age pouring over the wine list and finding things disappointing.

Immediately, Alex found him insufferable. A pale man with a weak chin who clearly thought his time was precious, but had thought nothing of keeping Alex and Gabriella waiting. Or of insulting the hotel staff with comments about the wine, while not bothering to make a formal introduction.

Alex made it a point not to telegraph any of his irritation to the other man. As soon as the wine had been selected, Alex turned his focus to the business at hand.

"Alessandro Di Sione," he said, extending his hand. "It's good to meet you, Prime Minister Colletti. This is my assistant, Gabby. A university student doing a bit of work experience. She's come with me to help me on my mission."

"And what exactly is that?" asked the prime minister, leaning back in his chair, his arms behind his head.

"I've become somewhat of an avid art collector of late. I heard that the collection here on Isolo D'Oro is beyond price. I'm interested in acquiring some pieces. Particularly those that belonged to the former royal family because of the…significance of the time period."

"A historian *and* an art enthusiast?"

"Absolutely," Alex said.

The other man smiled. "Which sorts of art are you most interested in?"

Alex hesitated. His grandfather was right. He probably *was* owed a refund on that expensive boarding school education.

"Portraiture primarily," Gabriella interjected. "Oils on canvas, mostly. Though I know that there are some excellent marble busts. And also some paintings that depict the scenery. Some wonderful depictions of farms? I have heard tell—I mean, Alessandro has told me. He is quite enthusiastic about the painting of the geese."

The prime minister laughed. "Yes. One of my favorites. I don't think I could part with it."

“Everything has a price,” Alex said.

“Some things.”

“Either way, we would be very interested in seeing the collection,” Alex continued.

“And I am happy to show it. The palace is home to the art collections of the royal family, so you’ll find whatever you like there. But I’m curious. You’re currently in charge of a vast shipping company, is that correct?”

Now, the other man was speaking Alex’s language. Alex leaned forward, suddenly feeling much more interested in the interaction. “Yes, I am.”

“I might have need of your services. The entire country might. It would be interesting to see if we can come to some sort of agreement.”

“Yes, that *would* be interesting,” Alex said.

It was suddenly clear why Prime Minister Colletti had been so eager to meet with them. Money. Alex’s very favorite language.

“Well, but we’re here to study art,” Gabriella protested.

“A good businessperson learns to multitask early on, as you will learn when you discover more about the world,” he responded.

She said nothing to that, but he could tell she wanted to kick him under the table.

“Wonderful,” the prime minister said. “It just so happens that I’m having an open house party at the palace. Celebrating fifty years of independence for Isolo D’Oro.”

He could feel Gabriella quivering with rage, and

for once, not all of it was directed at him. He reached beneath the table and quickly squeezed her hand. A warning.

What he hadn't anticipated was how soft her skin would be. How smooth.

He withdrew his touch quickly, keeping his focus trained on the prime minister.

"I would very much like to have you attend the party," the other man was saying. "Your assistant is welcome also. That way, you can see some of the art, a bit of the architecture and we can also discuss the possibility of a business partnership."

"That sounds perfect," Alex said, thinking it sounded anything but. A house party. Out in the country. It sounded like an awful costume drama. All they'd need was for the butler to murder somebody and for an elderly lady detective to show up and try to solve the crime.

"Excellent. We will discuss business over the next week. And until then we will just enjoy the dinner."

CHAPTER SEVEN

STANDING IN A hotel room and looking down at the magnificent views of Isolo D'Oro had been a magical moment for Gabriella. But it hadn't truly hit her until the limousine sent by Prime Minister Colletti rolled up to the grand estate that this was her *home.*

At least, in heritage. These magnificent, sprawling grounds should have belonged to her family. The beautifully appointed house with the magnificent stonework around the windows, the grand pillars and the arched doorway had been property of the royal family once. Until they had been driven out, banished from the nation that was in their blood.

For centuries, her ancestors had ruled. For centuries, they had inhabited these walls, walked through the gardens. Now, her grandmother couldn't even return to fetch a painting that held value to her that went far beyond money. Far beyond the attached history.

That was what struck her so hard, so deeply, as she walked through the front door, as they were led through the halls to the quarters in which they would be staying. This wasn't just history in the broad sense of the word. This was *her* history. Her family history. The blood of her ancestors might as well be in the stonework. Babies had been born here, the elderly had died here. Her people. Her ancestors.

It felt very personal. Almost painful.

And yet, at the same time, her heart felt swollen. She felt so connected to this place around her that it emboldened her. Filled her with a sense of confidence. Of belonging.

She had never felt so right before. As if this place was woven through her, a part of her she hadn't known she'd been missing.

All of that lasted for a spare few moments before they were shown to a magnificent suite with a small room off to the left. The tiny quarters belonged to her, the proximity of her room to Alex's of course intended to allow him easy access to her when he might need her to…assist him with whatever she was meant to be assisting him with.

Once the staff who had ushered them in was gone, Alex smiled. "It is comforting to know that if I have need of your services, you will be nearby," he said, looming large in the small doorway of her humble living quarters.

Her cheeks flamed. She knew that he didn't mean it in any kind of lecherous way, but for some reason her body insisted on interpreting it that way.

"After all," he continued, "you are my assistant. And I may well be in need of some *assistance* in the middle of the night."

She gritted her teeth, well aware that her cheeks

were glowing an incandescent pink. He could not be in denial about her thoughts. And she had a feeling that now he was just trying to wind her up.

"In case you need a glass of milk?"

"Yes." A wicked smile curved his lips. "I do often enjoy a glass of *warm milk* in the middle of the night. I find it helps me sleep."

"I'll be sure to give it to you early. The middle of the night for someone your age is what…eight o'clock?" She almost regretted taking that cheap shot. *Almost.* If only because it revealed the fact that she found him very disconcerting.

"Yes," he said, arching a brow. "Do bring it to me along with my vitamins."

Drat him. He wasn't even perturbed by that.

"I will do so, as you have requested, sir."

"I like that," he said, his voice a low rumble that rolled through her like thunder.

He had the ability to touch her, all through her body, without ever getting near her, and she couldn't quite understand how he managed it.

She wrenched her focus from him and looked around the modest room. Really, it wasn't bad. Everything was clean, and elegant. The walls were a mint green with white molding adding texture to them. There was no art in this room, but there was a lovely view of the gardens. And that, in her estimation, counted as art.

Alex moved away from the door and she followed him through, not quite sure why. She only knew that he seemed to draw her to him, like he was pulling her on a string.

She was too fascinated by it to fight it.

In contrast to her room, Alex's was sumptuously appointed. The walls had dark wood paneling and a great deal of classical art. There were floor-to-ceiling windows, but she couldn't tell what the view might be because the rich, velvet drapes were drawn over them. Then, in the back corner, there was a large bed with lots of fabric hanging from the ceiling, promising to seclude the sleeper from any unwanted light or noise.

"I don't think they've redecorated since the turn of the century. Last century," Alex said.

"Yes, I suppose this is all original. But that's part of the charm."

"Do you think? I find your perspective on things quite fascinating. You are a romantic."

She frowned. She had never thought of herself as a romantic before. She didn't think he was right. "I'm rather more invested in fact than fancy."

"So you say. But you are always delighted by the beauty around you. There is nothing terribly practical about beauty. And it isn't absolute. One person can find something beautiful when someone else finds it wholly unremarkable. Similarly," he said, speaking slowly, his dark eyes lingering on her in a manner that left her feeling hot, that left her feeling like he had touched her, "one can look at something every day for quite some time and never notice the beauty of it. Then suddenly, one day it might become beautiful to them. Beauty is strange that way. It hides in plain sight."

She swallowed hard, not quite sure why she felt like she was on fire. "I suppose the reverse is also true.

Beauty can be obvious. And as it proves itself to be nothing more than pale vanity it can lessen."

"Speaking of your mother and father?" he asked, the question bold and insensitive.

She supposed he was entitled, as she had been rather bold and insensitive herself when they had discussed his parents. "Yes. Does it remind you of yours, as well?"

"Very much."

"All right, I will concede then that maybe you're correct about me. I do like art. I do like frivolous things. Just not…the same kinds of frivolous things as some in my family."

"There is nothing wrong with enjoying the frivolous. I'm not even sure I would call it frivolous. Many people would argue that it is the beauty around us that makes life rich, don't you think?"

She nodded slowly. "I do agree. My life is very quiet compared to most people in my family. Really, it's very quiet compared to most people in my age group, I know. I live with an old woman and I suppose my habits are more reflective of hers than the average twenty-three-year-old. But I like it. I like to read. I like to listen to the sound of the rain on the roof. I like to watch the drops roll down the windowpane. I enjoy the quiet. I enjoy art for all that it doesn't tell us. For the fact that it makes us think and draw our own conclusions. I suppose I enjoy genealogy for the same reasons. We have to extract our own meaning from what we see before us and, from there, guess what the truth might be."

"A very interesting way of looking at it," he said, his tone different now.

"Is that how you see things?"

He shook his head. "I do not have much time for art. Or for books. Or for sitting and listening to the rain."

Her heart sank. "Oh. I thought... By the way you were talking..."

"I've lost the ability to appreciate beauty in the way you seem to. But it doesn't mean I don't appreciate your perspective."

"I suppose you are too jaded."

"Yes," he said, his tone taking on a rather black quality. "I suppose I am a bit too jaded. But then, living the sort of life I have, opulence all around me, my every whim, my every desire, so easily serviced, I don't know how I could be anything but."

"I've had a similar experience, don't forget."

"Yes, you seem to have practiced the art of self-denial a bit more successfully than I have."

"I don't consider it denial."

"Another of your virtues, I'm certain."

She frowned, walking slowly past him, pacing the length of the room, the marble floor clicking beneath her low-heeled shoes. She studied the paintings on the walls, depictions of the scenery around them. During another time. During other seasons. "My parents have indulged in everything imaginable, and yet, they still live life with a fair amount of excitement and passion. I want nothing to do with it. It looks exhausting. Dangerous. Selfish. But...for all their sins they aren't jaded. I feel they enjoy their excess, or they wouldn't continue in it. For you... You seem very bored. And I wonder why that might be."

"I think perhaps the problem with my life, Princess, is that I have seen where the road ends. There is desperate poverty in this world. Tragedies. And I know that there are those who believe that if they simply had one more *thing*, a little bit more money, they would find happiness. But my parents had everything. They had wealth. They had family. They had beauty. Sex, drugs and alcohol in every combination. They had everything. And they were never satisfied. They never stopped searching. They were hungry, always. When they should have been full. It was that continued searching that took everything beautiful they had in their lives and twisted it beyond reason. They had marriage. They had children. And yet, they went out and had affairs. My father made a child with another woman. A child that he never acknowledged. A child whose existence only hurt everyone involved. When you have so much, and yet you have no satisfaction. When you have so much and yet you must continue going until you destroy it all, I can only conclude that there was no happiness to be found in any of it. Not really. And so, I suppose having seen the end my parents came to I have trouble putting much hope in any of the things around me."

"You think it's pointless."

"I don't think it's pointless or I would have thrown myself off a building by now. I think there are aspects of life to enjoy. There is music I like. I enjoy my work. I certainly enjoy my money. I quite enjoy sex. But I'm not certain the satisfaction is to be found. I'm not certain that happiness is a thing that truly exists."

"That all sounds quite…hopeless."

"Maybe it is. Or maybe that's why I choose to take things in life with a healthy dose of cynicism. There are worse things, I should think."

"I think that there's happiness. I don't think that life is quite so meaningless as all that."

He lifted a broad shoulder and she was drawn to the way he moved. He was like a big cat, a predator. Lying in wait for his prey to make the wrong move. The one that would trigger the attack.

She had to wonder if she was the prey in this scenario.

"We all have our coping mechanisms," he said. "You have chosen to try and find satisfaction in the opposite things. While I have decided that I won't find whatever magic cure my parents were looking for within life's various debaucheries."

She paused in her pacing, turned to face him. "Do you think you'll find it anywhere?"

"I have my doubts."

"Do you believe in anything? Do you believe in love?"

He only looked at her, his dark eyes a bottomless well. "No."

"But you're here for your grandfather. Surely—?"

"I believe in fairness. I believe in faithfulness. I believe in keeping my word. As I told you before, I am a man who believes in business."

"Follow your head and not your heart, in other words."

"My head is the only thing I trust."

She let out a heavy sigh, looking back toward her bedroom. It was going to be strange, sharing such a close space with him. Last night in the hotel suite had been strange enough, but there had been a living area between their two bedrooms. This felt…rather more intimate. She should think nothing of it. It should be… nothing. That he was a man and she was a woman shouldn't matter because they wouldn't be engaging in any…man/woman things.

But it still felt strange.

"Then maybe you could use that very large head of yours to figure out how we'll find the painting in this enormous palace?" Her uncertainty, the fluttering in her stomach, made her feel cross.

"I could, I suppose." He tapped his chin as though he were thinking very hard. "The easiest thing to do would be to take a tour. It's likely the hiding place would be revealed to us during it."

"Sure. If only we could arrange that."

"Well, there will be tours. The biggest thing is that we can't turn the pockets of the place out, then leave with a valuable work of art. We have to appear to have come for reasons of business and pleasure. We have to stay. Anyway, I sincerely intend to work up some sort of trade agreement, so we will stay until the last evening party."

"There are parties?"

"Every night. He emailed me a PDF of the itinerary. Very helpful," he said, his tone dry. "But I think we should make sure to stay until the last party. Four days. Then we go. Easy."

Nothing about it sounded easy to her, not at all. To exist in this fishbowl playing a part she didn't know the lines for.

"Are you tired?" he asked. She had to wonder if he'd seen her sag beneath the weight of everything just as she felt it.

"Yes," she said, suddenly feeling exhausted down to her bones. That surge of strength, of certainty that she had felt when she first walked in, was gone now. Now she just felt wrung out. It was strange that coming to this place was so emotional. But it was. Enduring it all with this man who was so…intense, so very *present*—it only added to it.

"Perhaps you should get some rest. There is going to be a gathering tonight with the guests at the party. Appetizers and the like."

She frowned. "What am I supposed to do about that? I can't very well fix myself up. Here people know that I'm Princess Gabriella. Or they'll at least suspect."

"Then you won't fix up."

She scowled. "I like very much how this farce isn't damaging your vanity in any way."

"All of this was your choice, *Princess*. I for one am happy to create a bit of scandal. What do I care if the world thinks I've taken you to my bed? I don't care. Not at all."

"Yes, that is a charming perk of being male. You don't have to worry about rumors of your sexual promiscuity."

He chuckled. "I would guess you've never had to much worry about rumors regarding yours, either."

That goaded her pride. She didn't like him being quite so certain about that. "Perhaps I'm just discreet."

"Oh, I have no doubt that you are. You seem to me to be the very soul of discretion."

She sniffed. "I am. For reasons you should well understand."

"Go rest up. Then put on your armor of discretion and ready yourself for the party tonight."

CHAPTER EIGHT

AT THE MOMENT, no one would suspect Gabriella was a princess, as she was doing an excellent impersonation of a potted plant. She was all but hugging the back wall, dressed in a rather understated pencil skirt and a cream-colored top, complete with a single-string pearl necklace. Her dark hair was partly down, the front pulled back by a clip, the large glasses still fixed on her face.

She looked exactly as an assistant should. And yet, Alex found himself irritated by it.

The other women in the room were dressed in bright colors, saucy cocktail dresses designed to aid in the flaunting of their figures. Their hair expertly styled. And they were certainly not hanging on to the wall. He found that he wanted to see Gabriella without her glasses. That he wondered what it might be like to get a good look at her large, brown eyes. That he might like to see her full lips painted red.

And he knew he would like to see her figure in something designed to flatter it.

He would never be a very great appreciator of art,

but he was certainly an appreciator of the female form. And as such, he would simply like to see this one done up with a bit more finesse. That was all. All that discussion of beauty had been on his mind.

She wasn't talking to anyone, rather she seemed to be closely regarding the paintings on the wall. More than that, she seemed to be examining the molding, the floor, the baseboards, the wallpaper… She seemed to be having an entire love affair with the house.

Though he imagined that was to be expected. This was her ancestral home. She had never been here.

He imagined that must bring up all sorts of thoughts.

His family was originally from Italy, and he lived in America. But he had never felt displaced. Giovanni had often told him stories of how he had come to the US, how he had worked his way up from nothing to become one of the most successful men in the nation. Alex enjoyed going to Italy, but he supposed the point of it all was that he could. Yet, while in a technical sense Gabriella *could* have come to Isolo D'Oro, there would have always been a block of some kind. Her family hadn't left of their own accord. They had been banished. It was an entirely different circumstance. One that was quite heavy. And it seemed to be hitting her with its full impact.

"Alessandro Di Sione, right?"

Alex turned to his left and saw a shimmering blonde regarding him with her bright blue eyes. Now *this* was a woman who had taken great pains to flaunt every aspect of her beauty to its greatest advantage. The entirety of her potential was on display before him. There was nothing to wonder about. Nothing at all.

Except perhaps how she would look naked.

Though he had seen enough women naked to be able to guess. He studied her for a moment. He was so confident with his estimation of the size of her breasts without the cleavage-enhancing bra, of the color of her nipples based on her coloring in general, that he found he ultimately wasn't even curious.

"My name is Samantha," she said, smiling grandly, both realizing she'd lost him before she'd ever started. "I've followed your business exploits with great interest recently."

The way she said *exploits* left him in little doubt that it wasn't his business she had been paying attention to.

"Oh, have you?" he asked. "Perhaps you could tell me about them. I rarely pay attention myself."

She laughed, a high, sharp sound that shot down his spine like an arrow before ricocheting back up to the base of his skull. She touched his arm, leaning in closer. "I didn't know you were funny. I had heard you were frightening."

"Boo," he said.

She laughed again and he fought to keep from cringing.

He flicked a glance across the room at Gabriella, who was watching this interaction between himself and Samantha with what appeared to be great interest. She was now literally standing next to a potted plant, her hand closed around a leaf, her posture rigid.

He couldn't begin to guess what she was thinking. Couldn't begin to guess much of anything about her.

With Gabriella there were a great many unanswered questions.

"Really, we must make more time to get to know each other over the course of the week," she was purring now, all but arching into him like a very needy cat.

"What exactly brings you to the party?" he asked. He didn't care what her answer was. Not in the least. His attention was split between her and the little dark-haired woman with glasses standing against the wall. But he didn't think she noticed. She was far too involved in the performance she was putting on with him.

And he was too busy regarding Gabriella to listen to what she had to say. Which was a shame, really, for Samantha at least. He had a feeling she was putting her full effort into this. An intended seduction, or whatever nonsense she had in her head.

Strange, because in most circumstances he would be more than willing to take her up on the unspoken offer. But not now. He wasn't sure what it was. Perhaps the little bespectacled witch had cast a spell on him. He smiled ruefully, dimly aware that his companion Samantha had likely taken that smile as her due. And of course, it was actually owed to Gabriella.

Very strange. She wasn't the kind that revealed itself immediately. It was more like the sun shining through the trees as you drove down the highway. He would catch flashes of golden light before it faded away again into the darkness. But it was there. And when it struck him directly it was so intense, so brilliant, that it stopped him where he stood.

His eyes caught hers and held for a second before she looked down sharply, obviously embarrassed to have been caught staring at him. He felt no such embarrassment over being caught staring at her.

Then, suddenly, she scurried from the room, hugging the wall as she made her way to the exit.

"Excuse me," he said to Samantha. "I'm very sorry. I have to go."

He wasn't anything of the kind.

He set his drink down on a table as he left, exiting out the same door Gabriella had. He saw her turn left at the far end of the corridor, and he continued on down that way. Maybe she was just headed to the bathroom. Most definitely he didn't *need* to be following her. That didn't seem to stop him.

He had known from the beginning that it was her cleverness he would find to be trouble. He was not wrong.

Had she been boring he would never have chased her out of a crowded room while being talked to by a busty blonde.

But no, she did not have the decency to be boring.

She had to be interesting. She had to like books. And she had to explain things to him in funny, intricate ways that he would normally find incredibly arduous.

He was angry at her. And with each step he took he felt angrier. Because he was Alessandro Di Sione. He did not pursue women into empty corridors. But then, he also didn't go around hunting for old paintings, either. It was a week of strange happenings. It was entirely possible he should just embrace it.

He saw her head out one of the glass double doors and into the garden, and he followed suit. He said nothing as he walked along behind her in the darkness, heading down a gravel path through the garden. He wondered if she had any idea where she was going or if she was just following some sort of impetuous instinct.

She was a study in contradictions.

Quiet, and yet also very loud. She swore that she was practical, and yet he could sense that she was so much more than that. She was sensual. She enjoyed tactile pleasures. Visual pleasures.

He thought back to the way she had eaten dinner last night. How she had lingered over her wine. The way she had nibbled slowly at the fresh bread on her plate, and the appreciative sound she had made when she'd bit into the dessert she had ordered without hesitation.

There was no doubt about it; she was not an entirely practical person.

Damn her for being so fascinating.

The path curved, feeding into a clearing surrounded by hedges. At the center was a stone bench and he imagined that there were a great many flowers planted at various levels throughout. It was dark, so he could see nothing. Nothing but great inky splotches, breaking up the pale gravel.

Gabriella took a seat on the stone bench, planting her hands on either side of her.

"I do hope you have room on your bench for two," he said, moving closer to her.

She gasped and turned toward him, her wide eyes just barely visible in the dim light. “What are you doing out here?”

“Stopping to smell the roses?”

“You were deeply involved in a conversation when I left,” she said.

“Oh, yes. That. Remember our discussion about boring women?”

“Yes.”

“She was one.”

Gabriella laughed softly; the sound lifted high on fragrant air, mixing with the scent of flowers and winding itself around him, through him.

“How terribly tragic for her. At least she is beautiful.”

“I suppose,” he said. “Though I don’t think she knows she’s boring.”

“I guess that’s a compensation for the dull.”

“Such a comforting sameness.”

She scuffed her toe through the gravel. “It wouldn’t be so bad.”

“I don’t know about that. I think you would find it excruciating.”

She shifted, and he couldn’t make out her face in the darkness. “Do you think so?”

“Yes. I am completely certain that Samantha does not do genealogy in her spare time.”

“A loss for Samantha, then. But points to you for remembering her name.”

“I was only just speaking to her five minutes ago. I might be shameless, but my shamelessness has its limits.”

"Does it? You were talking to her like you were interested. But you looked...very bored."

"Did I? Perhaps I was simply looking down Samantha's dress and that's what my expression looks like in such situations."

"Unless you find breasts boring I don't think that's the case."

He laughed. He couldn't help it. He was shocked by the forthright statement. He felt he should know better than to be shocked by her small moments of honesty at this point. It was another of her contradictions.

She should be mousey. She should be timid. She should be utterly out of her depth with a man such as himself. And yet she handled everything he threw at her with aplomb, and never passed up an opportunity to shock him, which he would have said under any other circumstance was impossible.

"People are the same. Everywhere you go," he found himself saying as he walked over to the bench where she sat. "May I?"

She nodded slowly. "Sure."

He took a seat beside her, an expanse of empty stone between them. "These parties are the same."

"No, they aren't," she said. "How can they be? I once went to a gala at the most incredible castle. It was medieval and all the stonework was original. There was a chapel and I left the party to go explore—it was incredible. This place...it's full of my family history. I've studied it in books. But...being here is different. Books can't prepare you for the reality of something. It can only hint."

"I suppose to get all that out of a party you have to appreciate art, architecture and history."

"And you don't."

"I was mainly speaking of the people."

Of women who were looking to attach themselves to a man of wealth and status for short amounts of time. Of men who stood around touting their successes as they grew increasingly red-faced from alcohol and a lack of taking a breath during their listing of accomplishments.

"Yes, well. Places might have to be experienced in person to be fully understood. But books are better than people. In a great many ways."

"Is that so?"

"Yes. It's all written out in front of you, and even if you don't know what's going to happen…at least it's all there. Very certain. People aren't certain."

"I disagree. People are predictable. They want pleasure. They want to be important, to feel good. They want money, power. There are a limited number of ways they can go about obtaining those things. I find people extremely bland."

"I guess I just don't possess the insight you do," she said, sounding frustrated. "They don't make much sense to me at all. Those things they call pleasure…the things my parents do…they don't make them happy, do they?"

"And now our conversation circles back around," he said, pressing his palm flat on the bench, the stone cool beneath his touch. "So you live through books?"

"To an extent."

"Adventure stories?"

"Yes."

"Romance novels?" He was leading her now. Because he couldn't guess at her response. She was the one person who surprised him, and he found he wanted to keep being surprised.

She cleared her throat. "Uh. Not so much. The, uh, masculinity is all a bit...*rampant* in those."

"As one in possession of masculinity that might be considered rampant, I'm not sure what the issue is."

She sputtered, followed by a strange coughing sound. "I don't even know what that means," she said.

"You were the one who coined the phrase, not me. I think it's fairly self-descriptive. And I find well suited to me. A kind of masculinity that can't be contained."

"I think it makes it sound like a weed."

"A virulent one."

"I just... I don't find any of that relatable."

"Of course not. You don't possess rampant masculinity."

"I meant *romances*."

"I see," he said, something goading him to continue pushing her. To see where this conversation would go. He couldn't guess at her game. Couldn't read any calculation on her face, and not simply because of the darkness that shrouded them. "What exactly is it you find unrelatable?"

She paused for a moment, and when she spoke again, her voice was muted. "Well, he always finds the wallflower interesting, doesn't he?"

"Who?"

"The hero. He finds the strange girl fascinating. Wants to know more about her. Men don't. For the record, they *never* do. As you said, they like women boring. *You* like them boring. Or at the very least, they don't like them weird. Plus, there's all that racing heart, sweating palms business. Aching body parts."

"Your body parts don't…ache?"

She growled, a small feral sound. "That's horribly embarrassing."

"You're the one who brought us here," he said, lying. He had led the entire thing for just such a moment. "You can't get mad at me for building off it."

"I can get mad at you for whatever I like," she said, sounding completely regal again.

Silence settled between them. Finally, he spoke again. "We are, by the way."

"You are what?"

"We are fascinated by the wallflower. At least, I was tonight."

"You were not. You were bored."

"I was bored by the businessman who couldn't stop telling me about his portfolio. I was bored with Samantha. And I did not look down her dress. But you… You're the one person in that room that I couldn't predict. That I couldn't figure out. I had to follow you when you left the room because I had no idea where you were going, or what you intended to do. Very few people surprise me, Gabriella, but you do."

"I'm not sure how I feel about that. I'm not here to surprise you. I'm not really here to do anything to you. I'm just supposed to find that painting, which of course we haven't done yet. And I…I'm playing secretary to you and having to face the kinds of social situations I would rather eat a handful of bees than contend with."

"Well, don't eat a handful of bees. It sounds incredibly unpleasant."

"These kinds of things are unpleasant. Even more so when I look like this. At least when I have my team of people making me look…polished… At least then people are fooled for a few moments. Right now, my outside kind of matches my inside."

"Why is that a problem?"

"I just told you."

"I don't think that's all of it."

She shifted next to him. "I don't know. When I'm in costume—so to speak—at least when people reject me they're rejecting this strange version of me that isn't who I see in the mirror every day. Princess Gabriella is something I put on when I go out. But otherwise, I'm just me. And right now, it feels very much like all of those people out there ignoring me are rejecting real pieces of me."

"No one is rejecting you. It's my fault for having you come here as an employee. You are definitely being treated as such." He found that he felt a little bit contrite about the situation. And he was never contrite.

"That's my own set of issues, I suppose. I don't make very much sense, Alex. That's the real problem. I want to be left alone. I want to be anonymous. But… Not always. Not every time. Just once it would be nice to have a handsome man look at me and cross the room to be by my side."

"I'm not entirely certain whether or not I'm handsome, at least not by your standards, but—" he paused "—you're the one *I* crossed the room for tonight, Gabriella. Take that as you will."

Silence fell between them and she placed her hand flat on the bench, a few inches separating their fingertips.

"I suppose you did," she said, her voice unsteady.

"I could have had her," he said, speaking of Samantha. "But this was where I wanted to be."

"You're quite confident in yourself," she said, her voice trembling.

"Brought about by predictable patterns. I told you, people don't surprise me."

"I wish I had that confidence. I wish I wasn't so afraid."

She had no reason to be afraid. And in that moment he hated a world that bestowed so much confidence on the terrible and unworthy—on her parents and his. And robbed it from the truly unique.

He lifted his hand, placing it over hers, and feeling every inch a bastard for doing it. She was vulnerable, and by touching her at the moment he was taking advantage of her.

He wasn't sure whether he cared or not. He was accustomed to dealing with people who moved in common circles to himself. People who saw the world much as he did.

Gabriella was an entity unto herself. She was not an experienced woman. She didn't know this game.

Why are you even bothering to play the game with a woman you thought plain only forty-eight hours ago?

He didn't have the slightest idea.

He was equally confused by the idea that he had ever found her plain. She clearly wasn't. Not in the least.

"I find you impossible to predict," he said again.

"Is that… Is that a compliment?"

He was trying to process her words, but most of his brainpower was taken up with relishing the velvet softness of her hand beneath his. She was so warm to touch after the cold stone of the bench. So very much alive.

How long had it been since he'd had a woman? He couldn't remember. Because it was irrelevant. Whoever the woman was, whenever she was, she hadn't been Gabriella.

Gabriella, who seemed to be her own creature.

"Why are you touching my hand?" she asked.

"Because I want to. I have never seen much use in denying myself the things that I want."

"There are a host of reasons for self-denial," she said. "We both know that."

"Oh, I am better trained than my parents ever were. My desires don't come from errant passions. I'm a logical man."

"There is nothing logical about you touching my hand."

He moved his thumb slowly over her knuckles, stroking her. "No, I suppose there isn't. I suppose there is nothing logical at all in this."

There wasn't. He was touching her now, but it could never be more than that. Alex had few scruples, it was true. But he had some. He had limitations on his behavior, if only because he had seen what it was like when people didn't. His parents had cared for nothing.

He preferred life to be a series of business transactions. He only entered into transactions with people who had a similar amount of resources. He wasn't the kind of man who swooped in and killed off dying companies. Wasn't the type to offer seed money to a start-up. It just wasn't his way. He preferred everything equal. In terms both parties understood.

It was the same with his sexual liaisons. He had no interest in despoiling innocents. No interest in corrupting a girl who barely understood what desire was.

His stomach tightened, his body hardening at the thought. Calling him a liar.

Well, perhaps his body *was* interested, but that didn't mean he would act on it.

He had spent all of his life endeavoring to become a better person than his mother and father. To learn from the mistakes of that fateful night.

A little bit of errant arousal was hardly going to change that.

But still, he didn't move his hand.

"I think you're like me," she said, her words small, soft. "You say that you're logical. That you like business transactions. You play with people. You toy with them. You were doing it to Samantha back in the drawing room. You had no intention of ever taking her up on her offer, did you?"

"No. I didn't."

She shifted slightly beneath his touch and a surge of warmth shot from their point of contact straight down to his gut.

"But you let her think you might," Gabriella continued, her voice soft. "Right now, you're touching me and we both know that you'll never—"

She didn't get the chance to finish the sentence. Whether it was the challenge in her voice, the bold statement that he would *never*, or the softness of her hand beneath his, he didn't know.

Whatever the reason, he halted her words with his mouth against hers, kissing her hard, hard enough that he hoped it would make the wallflower bloom. That it would show she wasn't that wrong.

It was everything else.

But she was so warm, so soft, he forgot his goal almost immediately as it entered his mind.

She froze beneath his lips, her body stiff, rigid. She didn't return the kiss, rather she simply sat, motionless, shocked. She was soft. Indescribably so.

He moved away from her, his heart pounding heavily, his shaft as hard as iron. How long had it been since the simple meeting of mouths had had such a strong effect on his body? Since he was fifteen, sixteen? Perhaps never.

She hadn't even parted her lips for him. Hadn't softened beneath him. Hadn't succumbed in any way, and yet he felt as though he had just conquered the world.

"I should have taken her up on her offer," he said, his voice rough, gasping. "I should have wanted her.

I should be upstairs in my room, or in her room, having sex with her now. But I'm not. I didn't want her. I wasn't even tempted. No matter how much we might like it to be, desire isn't logical. Which means, at the moment, neither am I."

He stood up from the bench, needing to put as much distance between them as possible. He turned away from her, and even knowing he shouldn't, he spoke again. "All I know is that tonight I just wanted to cross the room to be with the wallflower."

CHAPTER NINE

HE'D KISSED HER. It was all she'd been able to think about last night, lying in bed with her lips—her *body*—burning.

It was all she could think about the next day, too. Which was ridiculous because they were on a tour of the stables. Which were fascinating from a great many angles—historical and equine.

But she was prickly and distracted. From exhaustion. From the heat of Alex's body next to her, from the night spent not sleeping.

Her jacket was itchy, too. Which didn't help. It was a pleasant day, warm and dry, the air blowing in off the sea. And she was wearing a jacket because Alex had said it was secretarial and that it was important she appear so because of reasons she had now forgotten since she had a bead of sweat running down the center of her shoulder blades.

Also she was still thinking about the kiss.

Ahead of them, one of the prime minister's employees was extolling the virtues of the groundskeepers, and the brave servants who had saved the facilities and all the horses during a fire that happened a hundred years ago.

"This is boring," Alex said, his lips brushing her ear as he leaned in to whisper to her. It sent a shiver down her neck, down her arm, caused heat to pool in her stomach.

She took a breath, realizing when she inhaled a healthy dose of his masculine scent that it had been a mistake. "Excellent," she said, taking great pains to keep her voice crisp. "A chance to see The Alessandro in his natural habitat."

"Are you observing me for a nature guide you are working on?"

"Rampantis masculinitis," she said, smiling slightly.

"Characterized by?" he asked.

She looked up at him, at the wicked glint in his eye, and she quickly looked away again.

The tour group had gone on ahead of them, and she had only just noticed that their pace has slowed dramatically. He'd acted like this was done with last night. Like he'd realized what a bad idea it was to encourage all of this…this stuff between them. But he was back in fighting form this morning.

He was deliberately keeping her back from the group. Keeping them both separate.

This really was like watching a nature show. The predator had separated the weaker gazelle from the herd. And after last night, she knew beyond a shadow of a doubt that she was the weaker gazelle.

"What are we doing?"

"I told you," he said, his smile turning wicked.

"I'm bored. Anyway, it wouldn't do to have you acting skittish around me, or to have me avoid you. You are my assistant, Gabby, not a bookish princess who all but forced herself into a treasure hunt with a stranger."

She looked ahead of the group, then looked up at him, at his dark, glittering eyes. There was an air of good humor about him, but there was something else, too. A base note that ran beneath it that spoke of danger, excitement.

She should turn away from it. She should have learned from last night. From letting him get too close.

She didn't. She hadn't.

"The painting," she said, her voice hoarse.

"Is not out here in the stables," he said. "I had hoped that we would tour the house today so we might get an idea of its location."

"Well, we can do a little bit of exploring on our own."

"I would like to do it during the day. I'm not sure where our host gets to during the daylight hours. He certainly isn't parading us about. But once the sun goes down, and the brandy comes out, he does seem to reappear."

"So, you think we should look for it at night?"

He lifted his shoulder. "It lowers the risk of running into him in the halls if we know he's socializing. It's either that or we tell him what we're after. But I have a feeling the cloak and dagger might be necessary. I told you, I'm willing to pay for the painting, but my fear is that he won't want to part with it when he understands what it is. That isn't an option. Money might be no object, but failure is unacceptable."

She nodded slowly. "Why do you want the painting so badly?"

"Because my grandfather wishes to have it. And I owe him a debt, I told you that already. He wants it—I will see he gets it."

She studied his expression. She could see that he had no attachment to the painting. He must love his grandfather. That she was certain of. Because Alex was not the kind of man who did anything that he didn't want to do. Only a few days in his presence and she was certain of that.

"What does it mean to him?" she asked.

"I'm not entirely sure. But there is a story..." He looked away from her, stared off toward the horizon line. "He has always told us this story, from the time we were children. About coming to America with nothing. He had eight objects that were dear to his heart. Objects that he had to sell slowly over the years to save himself from ruin. They were...they were very special to him. He often referred to them as his mistresses. Items that held sway over his heart. I don't know why. I don't know if it was because of their value, because of their beauty or because of their connection to another person. Regardless, these eight objects were the most important thing that Giovanni Di Sione possessed."

"The painting is one of them," she said.

"Yes. I was the last grandchild he asked. The rest have either been found or are being found by my siblings."

"But I don't understand how your grandfather could have come into possession of the painting."

"There are a great many possibilities. He could have bought it at an art auction of some kind, could have bought it off a merchant. And of course, your family could have bought it back and brought it to this house for safekeeping after the fact. I doubt there's any kind of serious connection."

She suspected that he didn't doubt it at all. She was beginning to suspect that there was some sort of connection between his grandfather and her family. And seeing as Alex wasn't stupid, she imagined he saw it, too.

"Or," she said, "he knew my grandmother."

"I'm certain your grandmother would have said something when she heard my name. At the very least, she might have thrown me out."

"What would throwing you out accomplish? As you pointed out, you didn't need either of us to retrieve the painting, not really. You're right, you could have flashed a little gold at my mother and you would have had all the information you needed."

"True. But still, I don't think there is much point in spinning a fantasy out of any of it. I know my grandfather. He is a good man. He raised us after our parents died. And before they died, he was our most stable influence. I've always cherished my time with him. He treasures his grandchildren. In a way that our parents never did. We were very lucky to have him. We are lucky to have him still. But I know we won't have him much longer. And that's why..."

"You need the painting." She looked up at the clear blue sky, blinking against the sun as the cool sea breeze ruffled her hair. "You love him very much."

He paused. "He's family. Of course I feel a great deal for him."

She smiled slightly, trying not to laugh at him, since she knew he wouldn't appreciate it. "Alessandro, I think you might have a heart."

He arched a brow and looked toward her. "Don't say that too loudly. We can't have any rumors about that getting around."

"Why? Would it destroy your reputation for being a monster? I have ample evidence that you aren't bad."

"Oh, really? Give me a few examples."

She sighed, letting out a breath and starting down a path that led back toward the estate, winding through a row of hedges that had bright pink flowers on them, little explosions of color against the dark green. She kept her eyes on those blossoms. A welcome distraction from Alex and his persistent presence.

"Well, you haven't breathed fire once since I met you."

"I've been taking antacids. It helps with that."

She laughed, the sound pulled reluctantly from her. "Okay, I haven't seen you gnawing on the bones of any villagers, either. In fact, I don't think any villagers have gone missing since we've arrived on the island."

"That's because I only eat royalty," he said, giving her a rather meaningful look.

She directed her gaze back to the flowers. "Also, you don't sleep in a coffin."

He reached out, grabbing hold of her arm and stopping her in her tracks. "How is it you know where I sleep? Have you been watching me?"

A rush of heat traveled up her arm from the point of contact with his hand and she blushed furiously. "Of course not. Even if I had looked into your room, you would have been shrouded behind the velvet curtains."

"Maybe I have a coffin behind them."

"I doubt it."

"All right, so maybe you have caught on to my secret. I'm simply a man."

"One who is going out of his way to help his grandfather. I think you might have a heart *and* a soul."

"My heart is hard as a rock and my soul is ever so slightly charred from walking through life's fires, but I suppose they're still there."

"You also didn't…" She looked away from him, regretting the words even as she began to speak them, but finding she was unable to stop them. "You didn't take advantage of me last night. You could have. Had you wanted to."

"I have no interest in taking advantage of maidens," he said, his voice hard.

Oh…oh, of course he didn't.

It dawned on her. Suddenly. Horrifically.

Of course he didn't have an interest in maidens. In her. Whatever madness had possessed him last night when he'd kissed her, it hadn't been attraction. Men like him simply weren't attracted to women like her.

To him, she was barely a woman. She was little more than a girl, and he made that very clear. Of course, she had made a similar number of comments about his age, and she didn't truly think he was old.

"I don't think you're old," she said, feeling the need to clarify it suddenly.

"Oh, that's excellent. I guess I won't dip into my retirement account just yet then."

"You're thirty-six?"

"Yes."

"See? Not even middle-aged."

He laughed. "Not even… You're a minx. Do you know that?"

She blinked, her heart suddenly beating faster. Stupid heart. He didn't want her. He didn't even like her. "I'm not trying to be."

"I'm sure that's true."

"You can let go of my arm now," she said, looking down at where he was still hanging on to her.

"What if I told you I didn't want to?"

"I would ask you why. And then I would ask you what good could possibly come of it."

Her heart was pounding so hard now she could barely hear herself speak. If he couldn't hear her heartbeat she would be surprised.

"You're right. There is no point. As I already told you, I'm not interested in defiling any maidens this week."

She pulled herself out of his grasp and continued on down the path. "Who said I was a maiden?" She closed her eyes for a second, allowing the sun to wash over her face, the corners of her lips curving up slightly into a smile.

"You didn't have to say it," he said. "I could feel it in your kiss."

Her stomach sank down to her toes and she opened her eyes again, the corners of her lips falling. "Was it so terrible?"

Of course it had been.

"Not terrible. Inexperienced. I could taste it on your skin."

"That's ridiculous. Inexperience doesn't have a flavor."

He grabbed hold of her arm again, turned her to face him, drawing her closely toward him. Rather than speeding up, this time her heart stopped beating altogether. He lowered his head slightly, then reached up, sliding his thumb along the edge of her lip. "Yes, Gabriella, inexperience absolutely has a flavor. And on your lips, there was also innocence and wildflowers. I did not mistake the taste of any of that."

He released his hold on her, put distance between them, and she still couldn't breathe any easier.

"You didn't taste like anything," she said.

"That's because you didn't taste me."

Prickles crawled up her back like an army of ants and she hunched her shoulders up around her ears, lowering her head and continuing on toward the estate.

"Suddenly, you don't seem to like honesty very much," he said.

"Suddenly, you're a bit too honest. You said—"

"I am bad at behaving, and I am terrible at restraint. Tell me you didn't like kissing me, and I won't bring it up again."

It would be easy to lie. All she had to do was open her mouth and tell him that she didn't like kissing him. That should be an easy thing to do. It should be a simple thing to make her lips form those words. But right now everything felt stuck. The words lodged in the center of her throat, curled up into a little ball, refusing to budge.

She said nothing; she just kept walking on ahead.

If he was triumphant over her silence, he didn't let on.

He was the one who broke the silence and it felt like a definite checkmark in the loss column for her.

"The party tonight is formal," he said, "everyone is going to be in their finest."

She let out a heavy sigh. "Except for me. In fact, I may skip this one and just sit in my little servant's quarters with a crust of bread and some cheese."

"That's quite dramatic. I think we could at least get you some fresh bread."

"There isn't any reason for me to go. Actually, I might be able to roam the halls a little bit if I stay behind."

"Hospitality has been extended to both of us. And I'm concerned about angering the host."

"Is that because of the painting or because you want to do business with him?"

"Everything is about business. I have an opportunity to increase my success while I'm here and I'm definitely going to take it. I don't want to do anything to compromise that. I certainly won't allow *you* to compromise it."

"Well, I don't want to be embarrassed."

"You didn't let me finish. The party tonight is a masked ball. That means everyone will be wearing masks."

"Thank you," she said, her tone flat. "I actually got that from the title *masked ball*."

"Just making sure."

"Well, there is still a problem with that."

"What's that?"

"I left my ball gown and my elegant face mask in my other luggage."

"I might not be royalty, *cara mia*, but I am a billionaire. I could acquire white tigers in the space of a couple hours if I wanted to. A gown and a mask will be no trouble at all."

"What if I would rather have the white tigers?"

"Your room is too small."

"They can sleep in my bed."

"I'm not getting you white tigers. It would only spoil you. Plus, then everyone would want one."

She couldn't stop the laugh that escaped her lips. She had no idea how he managed all of this. How he managed to make her feel hot, frustrated and amused in the space of only a few seconds. It was some kind of strange witchcraft she had never encountered before.

"Fine."

"*Fine* to the gown and the mask?"

She let out an exasperated sigh. "Would it matter if I said no, Alex?"

Suddenly, his voice seemed to be coming from closer behind her, his low, sensual tones skimming along her skin. "Not especially. If I had to I would go into your room myself and act the part of your valet."

"You aren't suggesting you would dress me?"

"I confess I have much more experience undressing women than I have dressing them. But I might be willing to make an exception."

It was official. She was going to burst into flame.

She had lied when she'd told him she didn't read romance novels. She did. Secretly. And while she pretended to snicker at them from behind her hand, the truth was she was fascinated. She had always been curious to know if attraction like that existed. If it was possible to look at someone and feel like they were touching you. Like it would be too much if they did. Like you would die if they didn't.

She knew it did now. And she knew it was the kind of intensity that fiction simply couldn't prepare you for.

His lips had barely skimmed hers last night and she had felt like the moon and stars had fallen from the sky and scattered around her in the garden, leaving the world upside down, glittering all around her, rather than in the distance.

But it didn't matter. She wasn't going to lose her head over him. That was the last thing she had told her grandmother. That she would not allow him to seduce her.

Her grandmother had warned her away from this kind of thing in vague terms, and when the subject of the painting had come up, just before they'd come to retrieve it, it had become clear to Gabriella why. Her grandmother had been wounded by a man such as this. One who was powerful, handsome.

One she was not meant to be with.

Quite apart from the fact that Gabriella couldn't imagine a future with a man like this, one who didn't believe in love, or commitment, she was a princess. And even if she didn't have a throne she would be required to make a certain kind of marriage.

It would not be to an Italian American businessman who had no pedigree. That just wouldn't do.

She blinked, trying to get a hold on her thoughts. The last thing he needed to know was that she was thinking about sex or marriage in connection with him.

"Well, there's no need for you to dress me. I will dress myself. But tonight we need to try and look for that room my grandmother spoke of. We need to try and find the painting."

"I agree with you. I think tonight might be the time we change the nature of this farce, don't you?"

"What do you mean?"

"I mean, we have established that you are nothing more than my assistant. No one suspects that you are Princess Gabriella D'Oro, and no one has any reason to. Tonight you will be wearing a beautiful dress, and your face will be covered by a mask keeping you from being recognized... When we slip away together a little bit early, it will hardly be suspicious. At least not if I have been holding you in my arms a little bit more closely than I have for the previous nights."

"What are you suggesting?"

"Tonight, you will play the part of my lover, Gabriella. There will be no scandal, and it will be the perfect excuse for us to slip away."

Her throat was dry, her heart pounding so hard she was afraid it might gain enough momentum to tumble up her throat and come spilling out of her mouth. "But I…"

"You don't know how? You don't know how to play the part of doting lover?"

Her cheeks flamed. "I have no worries about that. I can more than handle you, Alessandro."

"You see, when you say my full name like that, I become convinced that you are a bit more nervous than you let on."

"And when you take on that dry tone, I begin to suspect that you are a little bit more off-kilter than you like to let on. Perhaps it is *you* having a difficult time figuring out how you will play the part of my lover. But don't worry, I will be wearing a mask. So my looks shouldn't put you off."

"Did my kiss last night not prove to you that I don't find you unattractive?"

"The only thing your kiss last night proved is that you very much like playing games. But I don't like being the subject of them."

A man like Alessandro would never want a woman like her. With her large glasses and ill-fitting clothing—the only thing she had ever worn in front of him—her face devoid of makeup, he would never look twice at her.

Likely, he had seen her as a challenge, and he had set out to conquer her. Because that's who he was.

Well, she refused to be conquered.

"I have no problem playing the part of your lover tonight, Alex," she said, keeping her tone frosty. "But do not get any ideas about making it real. I understand what manner of man you are. I understand what motivates you. I am a source of amusement to you, as you have made very plain. I will not allow you to amuse yourself with my body."

Filled with a new sense of dignified rage, she stormed toward the estate. She had no idea why she was reacting this way. Had no idea why she hadn't seen all of this before. Had she truly imagined that he had been attracted to her? That the kiss had been genuine? That the rake had gone after the wallflower?

She was as much a fool for a beautiful face as her grandmother had feared.

As much a fool as anyone in her family was. Perhaps that was the curse. Her grandmother had fallen prey to a man. And had her heart broken by him. Her mother threw herself in front of men as though she were a willing victim and they were an oncoming train. Only to find herself tangled, destroyed, after each affair. Chipping away pieces of her marriage, pieces of herself.

Perhaps, in spite of all her attention to avoid such emotions, Gabriella should have truly known better.

She rushed through the estate, heading toward her room. Once safely inside, she closed the door and locked the connecting one between her room and Alex's. She would have to face him tonight. Tonight, she would have to pretend that she was his lover. She would need to fortify herself to cope with that.

She sat on her bed, breathing hard, anger, *hurt*, rising up inside of her.

But with a few breaths came clarity.

The only solution here would be to take control of the situation. Alex saw himself as above temptation, she knew that. He only gave in when he chose to. And of course, he didn't want her.

But tonight, she would *make* him want her. She would. She would turn the tables.

He would be the one left unsatisfied. He would be the one who didn't sleep because he was burning. But she would never give in to him. She would make him want her, and then, she would turn away.

She flopped backward onto the bed, a smile crossing her lips. She was incredibly satisfied with this new plan. With this vision for the future that put her much more in charge of things than she'd been previously. Yes, last night she had momentarily lost her head over Alex. And there were a few moments today when she had done so, as well.

But it would not happen again. If anyone was going to lose their head tonight, it was going to be him.

CHAPTER TEN

ALEX HAD BEEN dimly aware of the fact that Gabriella was a princess. He had originally fooled himself that she was not attractive, but now was exceedingly aware of the fact that she was beautiful. But what he had not realized was that, even behind the little gold mask that covered her eyes and part of her nose, her regal bearing would shine through.

What he had not realized was that, even with most of her face covered, her beauty would be undeniable. What he had not realized was that, in a designer gown that clung to her generous curves, she would be a temptation he was not sure he had the strength to resist.

He hadn't realized that manner of temptation still existed for him.

Her dark hair was left loose, styled in dark curls, full lips painted red, the only part of her face that was visible. Her dress was a bright blue, the neckline high, covering more of her golden skin than he would like. But it hinted at a figure more spectacular than he had thought it could be. It clung to her hips and thighs before flaring out at the knee and billowing about her feet.

She was, in truth, a much more elegant creature than he had ever imagined. It was like looking at a stranger, and yet someone familiar at the same time.

Then she took a step forward, turning her foot sideways, and tripping slightly on her heel. "Drat!" she said, straightening and fussing with the bottom of her dress.

He smiled, because there was the Gabriella he had grown to know over the past few days.

"You look beautiful," he said, the compliment rolling effortlessly off his tongue. She did look beautiful. She was *more* than beautiful.

"You don't have to say things like that," she said.

His chest tightened. He had wounded her earlier, and he bitterly regretted that. Still, he wasn't entirely certain it was bad if she didn't truly believe him attracted to her. He would never be like his father. He would never be the sort of man who simply took what he wanted without considering the feelings of others.

As a young man he had fixated on that little boy standing outside of the manor that night, the bastard child of his father who'd caused the car accident that killed his parents.

He had spent a great many years blaming that little boy. Hiding that little boy's existence. Something he bitterly regretted later on in his life. Something he had done his very best to make right. But it had been too late. Nate's life had been broken beyond recognition. Rejected by the only family he might have had, because of his birth.

Alex had brought Nate back into the family's life

when his grandfather had needed a bone marrow transplant and no one else had been a match. He hadn't regretted it, but he and his half brother had never made much of a relationship with each other.

As an adult his memory of the events of that night had expanded. Not just to his mother, and her distress. Not just to the boy. But to the other woman, who was equally broken. Who had been brought into his father's web somehow, who had born his child and received no support. Yes, more and more he thought about her. He thought about every single person who had been damaged by his father's selfishness. By his unchecked lust.

The more the years passed, the more he realized his father was the villain.

Alex was a great many things, but he refused to become that manner of monster.

And that meant he would never touch Gabriella. She was so very different than anyone he'd ever known. So untouched by the ugly things in the world. She had seen the way her parents had behaved, and she had managed to retain a kind of simple, open view of the world he could never remember possessing. She had retained her hope. He would be damned if he were the one to take that from her.

One thing was certain, while he might be able to give her physical pleasure, he would never be able to offer anything beyond that. Nothing more than pain.

His family was stuck with him. The damage to Nate was done.

He would extend that damage no further.

"Shall we go to the ball, Cinderella?"

He extended his hand and she looked at it as though it might bite her. "If I'm Cinderella," she said, keeping her hands fixed firmly to her sides, "does that make you my fairy godmother?"

"Never. Fairy godmothers are endlessly giving. They live to bestow gifts with no hope of receiving anything in return." He smiled. "I'm not so selfless."

"And what exactly do you hope to get in return for your gifts?"

"I'm getting it. Right now. As I told you, you look beautiful."

He could see pink color bleeding beneath her skin, spreading outside the edges of the mask, revealing her blush to him. Reviewing the pleasure she took in his compliment. "And you… You look like the Phantom of the Opera."

He touched the white mask on his face. "That's kind of the point."

"Except you aren't hideously scarred."

"My scars are metaphorical in nature."

"The same can be said for most of us, I suppose. Though scarring is kept to a minimum when you spend most of your time in the library."

"I knew my lack of a library would become problematic one day."

"Right now, the only problem we have is a lack of a painting," she said, gently steering the conversation back to the reason for all of this.

She was good at that. He was losing the plot. Completely. For a moment he had forgotten that he had a goal that extended beyond dancing with her tonight.

A goal that went past seeing her in this gown and that mask.

Time moved a strange pace here. It was slower. Being away from his phone, his desk, being outside of his world, was doing strange things to him. He wasn't entirely certain he disliked it.

"Then I suggest we get a move on. The painting will wait for no man. Except it has done exactly that for the past fifty-plus years."

This time, she did take his hand. And he was the one tempted to pull away. From the heat. From the silken quality of her touch. He didn't. He was the experienced party. The touch of a woman's hand against his should not be cause for any reaction whatsoever.

He knew that. Repeated it over and over as he led her from their quarters down the long hall and toward the ballroom.

No matter how committed he was to understanding it on an intellectual level, he could not convince his body to agree.

So he did his best to concentrate on the feeling of his feet making contact with the marble floor. One step, then another. When he focused on that, the burn, where her skin made contact with his, lessened.

A bit.

They approached the doors to the ballroom and two elegantly appointed staff, not wearing masks, opened the double doors for both of them. "I feel like I should bow," he said, leaning in to whisper the words in her ear. "But at my age it might be bad for my back."

She looked up at him, dark eyes glinting from behind the mask. “Stop that.”

“But it’s so much fun.”

She rolled her eyes and he led her into the ballroom where couples were already dancing. “This room… It’s amazing,” she said, looking about them at the high, painted ceiling before her eyes fell to the pale walls, made ornate by sconces and crisp white molding.

Nothing about the designer dresses the other women were wearing. Of course not. Gabriella preferred art and architecture. Always.

“Gabby,” he said, drawing her attention back to him. She didn’t look nearly as annoyed as she typically did when he used the nickname. She looked… There was something strange in her expression. Something he feared he understood. Something he wished he hadn’t seen. “If you keep staring at the walls with more admiration than you afford me no one will believe it when we slip away.”

He led her deeper into the ballroom, toward the dance floor, and her attention drifted from him as she continued to stare at the walls, at the art, probably at particularly historically significant dust motes, knowing her.

“That could be a problem,” she said, distracted.

“Yes. One I will correct.”

He chose that moment to pull her into his arms, into a closed hold. Her attention snapped back to him. “What are we doing?”

“Dancing,” he said as he led her into the first step.

"So we are," she said, one hand caught up in his, the other resting on his shoulder.

She curled her fingers in a fist, as though she were afraid to touch him too much so she needed to minimize the amount of skin making contact with his jacket.

"I feel tonight we might be very rude."

"Will we?"

"Yes. We should socialize with everyone. You should approach the women and ask them who they are wearing and I should try and forge as many business connections as I possibly can with everyone in attendance. But I'm not going to. And neither are you. Because tonight we are only going to look at each other. We are only going to stay for the minimum amount of time and we're going to make the world believe that I could not wait one more moment to have you in my arms."

He could feel the breath leave her entire body, could feel her limbs go stiff. "I'm in your arms right now."

"No. Not like this. It would be different."

"How?" she asked, her voice a hushed whisper, her dark eyes full of fear, curiosity and excitement.

"It would be different because we would be alone. Because if there was nothing around us but all of these beautiful walls and I were to take you into my arms you would know that there were no limits to what might happen next. Everything would be different. It would be quiet, there would be no music. Only our breathing. The air around us would be different."

She swallowed visibly. “That’s what…that’s what everyone will think is going to happen?”

“Yes. By the end of this dance no one will be in any doubt that the moment I have you alone we will not be discussing art, let alone looking at paintings.”

He drew her closer as the music changed, not releasing her between songs, but rather continuing to sway gently with her. “But we are,” she said, “looking at paintings.”

“Of course,” he said, never taking his eyes from her. “Touch my face, Gabriella.”

“Wh-what?”

“I want you to lift your hand from my shoulder, and rest your palm against my face. I want you to take your fingertips and trace my jaw, down to my chin, then bring your hand to rest on my chest.”

“Why?” she asked, her expression almost frantic.

“It’s for the painting.” He ignored the dull beating of his heart—it was for a lot more than that. That reminded him there were other ways to do this.

She obeyed his command, even while her expression remained frightened. Soft skin made contact with his face, the light drift of her fingertips along his cheek, down his jaw and then, just as he had told her to, she brought it to rest against his chest. He was certain that she could feel his heart, beating hard beneath her palm.

He never took his eyes off hers as he slipped his arm slowly from around her waist and reached for her wrist, curling his fingers around it and drawing her hand to his lips, pressing a kiss to the center of her palm.

“That wasn’t… You didn’t…”

He released his hold on her, raising his hand to capture her chin between his thumb and forefinger. “I suppose I didn’t. How many ‘Hail Marys’ do you suppose I have to say to atone for that?”

“I don’t know,” she said, her voice raspy, scraped raw.

“It has been longer than I care to remember since my last confession. But for you, I would gladly get on my knees.”

Gabriella straightened, as though bolts of lightning had just shot straight down her spine, as though she had been hit with a thought so real, so strong, it had manifested itself physically. “You’re very good at empty flirtation, Alex.” She moved her arm around his neck, placing her fingers on his skin. “I wonder what might happen if you had to make good on any of your promises.”

“Why don’t you try to hold me to them, Gabriella?”

“Say something real,” she said, moving closer to him, slowly, as though it were taking great effort for her to move nearer to him, as though it took everything she had in her to keep herself from running away. “You’ve been playing a game with me from the moment we met. So now, if you want this to go on, I want you to tell me something and I want you to say it without that mocking gleam in your eye, or that wicked curve to your mouth. I want you to be real for one moment. Just one.”

“And what do I get in return?”

“Whatever you want.”

He could tell that the words had left her lips before

she had given them her full permission. He could also tell that she wished she could call them back.

"A very dangerous gift to offer to a man like me."

"I have no doubt." But, to her credit, she didn't rescind the offer.

"A real kiss for a real confession," he said, "it's only fair."

"All right," she said, her words breathless.

"You are beautiful," he said, keeping his gaze locked with hers. He kept his grip on her chin tight, didn't allow her to look away. "Quite apart from this quest, this game, apart from…me. The fact that no one has ever told you before, or at least has never made you feel it before, is a crime unspeakable in its cruelty."

She blinked, relaxing in his hold. "I… I don't know what to say. No one has ever… No one has ever said anything like that to me."

"You were very angry yesterday. I… The way that I dealt with you was wrong. I hurt you. It was not my intent. You are sweet, Gabby. I am a man who licks the sugar off sweet things and leaves them discarded. But even if I shouldn't say this, I want you to understand that while we might be here putting on a show for others, while I may have confessed to you my boredom with life, the attraction I feel for you is separate from that."

She took a deep breath, her eyes fluttering closed, and then, her hands still curved around the back of his neck, she stood up on her toes and pressed a kiss to his mouth. It was quick, short, but he felt branded by it. Was certain that she had left a crimson stain behind from her lipstick, but something deeper than that. Something permanent.

"Now," he said, "I think it's time for us to excuse ourselves."

Gabriella had failed in her objective. And she wasn't entirely sorry about it.

She was supposed to seduce him. She was supposed to flip the tables on him. But from the moment she walked out of her room wearing that dress, she had felt like putty. Particularly when he looked at her, with all that heat and masculine energy radiating from him. He certainly looked like a man not entirely indifferent to what he saw before him.

And that, she supposed, was the variable she hadn't counted on. The fact that coming close to seducing him might seduce her right back.

Then there had been the touching. Her touching his face, him kissing her hand. She had felt very much the frustrated mouse in the paws of a cat that wasn't really hungry, just looking for amusement.

That was when she'd remembered herself. When she'd realized she was failing at her own objective. And so she had tried a different approach.

Yet again, he had come out on top. She had turned to nothing more substantial than spun sugar when he complimented her, then she'd nearly lost her nerve when she'd kissed him. Then she nearly dissolved when his lips had touched hers.

She was not a very good seductress. That was just the truth.

But…it turned out she was eminently seducible. Beautiful words from a beautiful man that touched her down deep beneath her clothes, beneath her skin, changed everything around inside of her. Made her forget to protect herself.

The wing of the palace they were in now was completely empty of guests or staff, it seemed. Everyone was in the ballroom, or on the other side of the house wearing a path between the kitchen and the ballroom.

"Come with me," he said, wrapping his arm around her waist and moving at a brisk pace toward a set of double doors at the end of the corridor.

She did. Because this was the game. Because there was nowhere else she wanted to be. And after tonight it was over. This hunt. This flirtation. Whatever it was.

The only flirtation she'd ever had in her life.

The thought made her want to cry. Sit and weep in the middle of the corridor. But she couldn't do that because they were on a painting quest.

She hoped it took all night.

That they could spend the whole evening wandering through vacant halls on a quest, and if he never touched her it would be okay. It would be okay as long as she was walking with him.

Are you that easy? A few compliments and you're ready to melt all over him like butter.

Yes. She was.

But the strange thing was, she knew Alex now. And she knew that what he'd said in the ballroom was real. What she didn't know was what it meant for him, for them, and for the ticking clock that was winding down to midnight, when the enchantment would break and Cinderella would go back to being a bespectacled bookworm beneath his notice.

He opened one of the doors and slipped through the crack, bringing her with him, before closing it behind him.

"Do you suppose he has some kind of security camera system?"

"Not that I've noticed," Alex said. "And believe me, I've been keeping my eye out. But he has no reason to think that any of the guests are going to make off with the art. And we're not going to make off with any of the art that he knows about."

"A fabulous technicality."

"Speaking of technicalities, I want my kiss," he said, turning to her, his expression suddenly hard, like granite.

The breath rushed from her body. "I kissed you," she said. "Already, I mean."

"You kissed me in front of everyone else. You wanted real words for me, and I want a real kiss from you. That kiss always had to happen for the two of us to excuse ourselves from the ballroom. I want one that isn't inevitable."

"Is that so?"

"Though I'm beginning to wonder if a kiss between the two of us was always inevitable."

She laughed, a shaky, breathless sound. "Since when? Since you first walked into my grandmother's house when I was barefoot and in my glasses?" She wished it were true. She wished he had.

"Yes."

"That doesn't make sense."

"It doesn't. You're right. Nothing about this makes sense." He was the one who closed the distance between them, who reached out and curled a lock of her hair around his finger before letting it fall free. "I'm not certain it matters."

"It should."

"There are a lot of *shoulds* in the world, Gabby. But they very often become *shouldn'ts*. There isn't much to be done about it. Except perhaps do the one thing that feels right."

She didn't know if this felt right. No. It didn't feel right. It felt wrong. Very, very wrong. But she still wanted it. That was the thing.

She took a sharp breath, taking a step in toward him, pressing her hand to his chest. She looked up at his eyes, hard and dark, his expression still mostly concealed behind the mask. She flexed her fingers, scrunching the stiff white material of his shirt, then smoothing it again, relishing the feeling of his heat, his hardness, beneath the fabric. He was so different than she was. She had never truly fully appreciated just how different men and women were. In a million ways, big and small.

Yes, there was the obvious, but it was more than that. And it was those differences that suddenly caused her to glory in who she was, what she was. To feel, if only for a moment, that she completely understood herself both body and soul, and that they were united in one desire.

"Kiss me, Princess," he said, his voice low, strained.

He was affected.

So she had won.

She had been the one to make him burn.

But she'd made a mistake if she'd thought this game had one winner and one loser. She was right down there with him. And she didn't care about winning anymore.

She couldn't deny him, not now. Not when he was looking at her like she was a woman and not a girl, or an owl. Not when he was looking at her like she was the sun, moon and all the stars combined. Bright, brilliant and something that held the power to hold him transfixed.

Something more than what she was. Because Gabriella D'Oro had never transfixed anyone. Not her parents. Not a man.

But he was looking at her like she mattered. She didn't feel like shrinking into a wall, or melting into the scenery. She wanted him to keep looking.

She didn't want to hide from this. She wanted all of it.

Slowly, so slowly, so that she could savor the feel of him, relish the sensations of his body beneath her touch, she slid her hand up his throat, feeling the heat of his skin, the faint scratch of whiskers.

Then she moved to cup his jaw, his cheek.

"I've never touched a man like this before," she confessed.

And she wasn't even embarrassed by the confession, because he was still looking at her like he wanted her.

He moved closer, covering her hand with his. She

could feel his heart pounding heavily, could sense the tension running through his frame. "I've touched a great many women," he said, his tone grave. "But at the moment it doesn't seem to matter."

That was when she kissed him.

She closed her eyes and leaned forward, pressing her lips to his, her heart thudding against her chest so wildly she could hardly breathe. She felt dizzy. She felt restless. She felt…everything.

It was the most natural and comfortable thing in the world to be in his arms. And also the most frightening. The most torturous.

She felt as though she'd come home, as though she'd finally found a place to rest. One that was hers and hers alone. But it wasn't enough. And it never would be. His suit and her gown put too many layers between them.

Her title and his lack of one.

His age and experience coupled with her relative youth and inexperience.

Thirteen years. Thousands of miles. Lord knew how many women.

An unbridgeable divide, but one that was reduced to nothing as she stood here, tasting him. Savoring him. Holding him.

There was no space between them now. None at all. They were both shaking, both needing, both wanting.

She curled her fingers into a fist, holding him tightly as she angled her head. Then she jolted when he parted his lips, his tongue tracing the seam of her mouth, requesting entry.

She couldn't deny him. Not now. Possibly not ever.

He wrapped his arms around her, enveloping her, holding her close. One hand pressed between her shoulder blades, the other sliding low, just low enough to tease the curve of her buttocks without actually going past the line of impropriety.

Her world was reduced to this. To his hands, his lips, his scent. His every breath. If they had come into this room for anything other than the kiss she didn't remember it.

If there was anything beyond this room, this moment, this man, she didn't remember it, either.

They parted slowly, so different from that kiss in the garden. This felt natural, even though she regretted the end. They were both breathing hard, both unsteady. She lifted her hand and touched his cheek, felt the rasp of his whiskers beneath her palms, drank in the sight of him. What she could see of him that wasn't covered by the mask, anyway.

"We should look for the painting," she said, knowing she sounded dazed.

Her lips felt hot. Swollen. She wondered if they looked different, too. She couldn't possibly have any lipstick left on them—that was certain.

"Painting?" he asked, the corners of his mouth turning up.

"Yes," she said, her tone dry. She cleared her throat and started to walk toward the back wall. "She said there was a painting in one of the rooms, and only I could open it..."

"The key," he said.

"Yes. I'm good at keeping secrets, it turns out. All

those years of not having very many people to talk to, I guess."

She reached beneath the neckline of her gown and fished the necklace out, holding it up in front of her.

"The key," he said, his tone slightly different than it had been a moment earlier.

"Yes. It fits into a frame. She said it was scenery. Of a farm."

"There's a lot of that here."

"I know," she said, moving closer to the far wall and examining the different scenes in front of her. "They really do like their geese," she muttered as she moved down the row, examining the frames, looking for any evidence that one might not be a typical picture. "There are some farm scenes in here, but nothing quite like what my grandmother described. I feel like this is the wrong room. The sorts of farmhouses my grandmother described were from a slightly different era. They predate these more modern houses."

"Do they predate the geese?"

"There were always geese, Alex," she said, enjoying the way his words played off her own. A thrill the way their lips worked together, even when they weren't touching.

"Then let's keep looking," he said.

He took hold of her hand and another thrill shot through her as he led her from the room and back down the hall. He opened another door.

"What sorts of paintings are those?" he asked.

She looked in, her heart pounding hard due to the excitement. Sort of. Mostly it was the proximity of Alex.

"Cityscapes," she said, "it won't be here."

They continued through a room filled with the portraits of royals, and one with scenes of the beach. Finally, they opened up a door to a room with a wall lined with paintings of farms. Pale, rosy cheeked children with animals, thatched roof homes and, well, more geese.

"It would be here," she said, "I'm sure. So now… we just have to figure out which. Which painting looks different? Which one might be a false front?"

Alex squinted looking around the room. Then his posture went straight as though a realization had shot through him like a lightning bolt. "Here," he said.

She turned to look at him. He'd stopped in front of a painting with a farmhouse, and a young girl in front of it. His fingertip was pressed into the corner of the frame.

"What is it?" she asked.

"There's a small…a notch here in the corner. Look."

She moved over to where he was and her mouth fell open, her fingers trembling as she held the charm on the necklace out in front of her. "I think… I think this is it," she said.

He moved aside and she stepped forward, pressing the back of the necklace into the notch and pushing it in. The frame popped away from the wall about two inches and Gabriella stood back, bringing her necklace with her.

She stared at the picture for a moment, then looked over at Alex. "Well, now I'm nervous," she said. Her stomach was flipping over, her hands sweating. She was…excited. But terrified. If the painting was there… who knew what would happen. If it got out and it created more waves for her family it would be disastrous. She would never be able to salvage their reputations. Not even with a more complete and fair history compiled.

But if it wasn't there…

She had wondered about the painting for so long. If it was real. And now they knew it was real and the possibility of seeing it…

Alex swung the painting open and revealed a large rectangle behind it, set deep into the wall, covered in burlap.

"Oh," she breathed, "that could be… I mean, it probably is…"

Alex reached out and grabbed hold of the burlap, drawing it down to reveal the painting underneath.

"Well," she said, "you kind of took the drama out of it."

"You don't think this is dramatic enough?" he asked.

It was. Even without fanfare. Because lowering the burlap had revealed what could only be *The Lost Love*. It was a woman, sitting in front of a vanity, hands in her dark curls as she gazed into the mirror. She was naked, her bare back on display, the suggestion of her breasts in the reflection of the mirror. She was seated on a cushion, the curve of her bottom visible.

It was…provocative, certainly. But beautiful. And hardly the salacious, distasteful scandal the press had insinuated it might be so long ago.

"And this is why..." she breathed. "This is why we search for the truth. There's nothing... There is nothing filthy about this. Nothing wrong with it."

"I'm inclined to agree. But then, I am a fan of the female form."

She turned to look at Alex. "I only mean that the media made it sound as though revealing this photo would be detrimental to my grandmother's reputation. Certainly..." She looked back at the painting. "Certainly, it suggests that she was intimate with the painter. It is not a standard sort of portrait that one might sit for. And someone in her position was hardly ever going to pose nude. Plus... There's something... There's something more here than you see in a portrait that simply contains a model. The painter was not detached from the subject. I can feel it in every brushstroke. There's so much passion."

Her fingers reached out to the corner of the painting, where the artist's initials, *B.A.*, were faintly painted.

"Or," Alex said, stuffing his hands in his pockets, "he was a very good painter."

"It was more than that, Alex."

"It makes no difference to me. My job is simply to bring the painting to my grandfather."

Gabriella frowned. "Why does your grandfather have more of a claim to this than my grandmother? It's her in the painting."

"Yes, it is. But my grandfather owned this painting at one time. He will be willing to pay whatever price is fair. It was not your grandmother's dying request, but it is his."

"We will bring it back to Aceena. She wants to see it. At least give her that."

"I can't be away from work indefinitely, Princess," he said.

She looked at him, unable to make out the finer points of his expression behind the mask. "Please. Let's bring it back to her."

He regarded her closely for a moment. Then he nodded slowly, moving over to where the painting was, extending his hand and brushing his thumb along the edge of the canvas. "It is very beautiful. In fact," he said, looking away from the painting and back at Gabriella. "It reminds me a bit of you."

Her face heated. "I don't look anything like that."

"You certainly do. Beautiful. Lush."

"I don't."

"This painting is not the view of the subject. It's the vision of her admirer," he said, his dark eyes locked on to hers. "For that reason, I would say that I'm in a much better position to evaluate it than you."

"You're not my lover," she said, the word sweet and thick like honey on her tongue.

"No," he said, his tone taking on a wistful quality. "I'm not."

"How are we going to get this back to our room?"

"Very quickly," he said.

He took the portrait out, covered it with the burlap again and quickly closed the original painting.

She moved forward and pressed her necklace deeply into the notch again to lock it just as before.

"If he truly had no idea this painting was here, he

will have no reason to believe it isn't mine," Alex said. "Of course, carrying a rather large canvas through the house may arouse suspicion. I doubt I could convince him I was simply taking the painting out for a walk."

"Then we had better hurry," Gabriella said. "Everyone else is still occupied in the ballroom."

"And thank God for Prime Minister Colletti's devotion to having a good time."

They walked to the double doors that led back to the corridor. Alex opened the first one slightly, peering out into the hall to see if anyone was there. "It looks clear," he said.

She nodded, and they both slipped through the outside, closing the gallery door tightly shut behind.

It was ridiculous. Alex was wearing a suit that was rather disheveled, they were both masked and now Alex was also carrying a piece of art.

If anyone saw them, they would likely imagine they had simply had too much to drink.

They walked down the hall quickly, then they rounded to the left and froze. Up against the wall was another couple engaged in the very thing Alex had wanted the rest of the party to believe *they* were engaged in. The man had the woman pressed tightly against the wall, her hands held over her head while he kissed her again, his other hand roaming over her curves.

A flash of heat wound itself around Gabriella, her entire body ready to go up in flames at the sight of it.

What would it be like to have Alex unleash his passion on her like that? To have him press her up against the wall. To have him touch her like that.

The scene before them highlighted just how circumspect he had been.

For some reason, she was disappointed.

“Quietly,” Alex whispered as the two of them continued behind the amorous couple. The woman’s eyes were closed, the man’s back to them, and they were able to walk along behind them without detection. They hurried through the halls, the rest of which they found empty. Not stopping until they reached their rooms.

“Excellent,” Alex said, closing the door tightly behind them. “I will pack this away, and if anyone looks through my suitcase I will say that I acquired it elsewhere during our travels. There is no reason for them to think otherwise.”

Gabriella shook her head, laughing—a husky sound. “I never imagined in my wildest dreams that I would be involved in an art heist.”

“Does it not belong to your family, Gabriella?”

“I feel it does,” she said.

“Then it’s hardly a heist.”

“Still. I’ve done quite a lot today that I never imagined I would.”

Dancing with him. Kissing him. Being called beautiful. Now it was ending. This was the end of it all. She didn’t care about stealing the painting. She cared about the mission being over.

“I have to say the same, Gabby, and I did not think that was possible.”

She wasn't even irritated this time when he called her Gabby. No one else called her that. It was a name that only came from Alex. And she decided that there was something she quite liked about that. Whether it was because it kept this entire event separate from her real life, or because it made all of this feel special.

She was desperate to feel like it was special to him.

"I'm glad you found it diverting."

He laughed. "Oh, I found it more than that."

He took his mask off then, reached up and loosened his black tie. There was something about that look. That rakish, disheveled look that made her heart beat faster. That made her limbs feel weak. That made her stomach tighten.

Of course, it was the same when he was perfectly pressed, the same when he had a mask over his face. It was the same no matter what.

"We will leave tomorrow," he said.

"What reason will we give?"

"I will tell him that urgent business has come up in the States. I think I have done enough to secure a deal with the prime minister, and I managed to get what I came for. All in all, quite a successful trip."

Gabriella couldn't help but laugh. "Almost too successful. I keep expecting guards and hounds to descend upon us."

"Nothing like that, I think. I'm not sure this painting is truly valuable to anyone other than our grandparents."

Gabriella blinked, pulled up yet again by the link between Lucia and Giovanni. "Yes. It's very strange, that."

"Not especially."

"A bit."

"Only if you like romanticizing things. And I do not."

She rolled her eyes. "How very surprising."

He paused in front of her, a strange expression passing over his face. The left side of his lips curved slightly upward as he studied her. He moved forward and her breath caught in her chest.

He reached out, tracing the edge of her mask before lifting it slowly. He pulled it away, the soft brush of his skin against hers enough to make her feel like she was on fire. "So very beautiful," he said, his words hushed.

She waited for him to lean in. Waited for him to kiss her again. But he didn't. He simply stood, looking at her, not touching her, not making a move to close the distance between them.

She wished she were brave. Brave enough to touch him. To lean into him. To recapture what had happened in that empty room.

"Goodnight, Gabriella," he said finally, his words summarily dismissing her, stealing her chance at bravery.

She cleared her throat. "Goodnight, Alex."

She turned and walked into her bedroom. She felt very much like she had missed something. Like she had left a very important piece of herself behind.

She blinked hard against the stinging sensation in her eyes, did her best to breathe around the rock that had settled on her chest.

They would leave tomorrow. They had completed their objective. Tomorrow, she would be back on Aceena. Back with her grandmother. And everything would return to the way it was.

CHAPTER ELEVEN

EVERYTHING HAD GONE smoothly during their escape from Isolo D'Oro, and it continued to go smoothly upon their reentry into Aceena. Alex would have been surprised, but things tended to go smoothly for him, so he saw no reason this should be different. Except for the fact that everything about it felt different in a million small ways he could not quite quantify.

Well, there was one thing that he could name. Gabriella. He ignored that thought as they walked into the hall at the D'Oro estate.

He had the painting under his arm, the rest of their bags being handled by the staff. Gabriella was walking along beside him, wearing a pair of plain pants and a button-up blouse, her very large glasses returned to their usual position. And somehow, even with all of that, he saw her no differently than he had last night. She was fascinating, beautiful, irresistible. But here he was resisting. Overrated, in his opinion.

"We must bring this to my grandmother as quickly as possible," Gabriella was saying, the animated tone of her voice never failing to stir something inside of him.

She cared about so many things. Dusty books and history and the people around her. It made him ache. Made him wish he could still feel like that. Feel in ways he hadn't since he was eleven years old.

They were directed by the staff to the morning room, where her grandmother was taking her tea.

"Grandmother," Gabriella said, the word sounding more like a prayer than anything else. As though Lucia were Gabriella's salvation, her link back to the real world.

He still didn't feel linked to the real world. The shipping company was back in New York, along with a great many of his real-world concerns. Somehow, over the past week, his life had started to revolve around a painting, and giving compliments to the woman that stood before him.

"Is that it?" Lucia asked, gesturing to the painting that Alex held, facing away from her.

He nodded slowly.

"May I?" she asked, her voice suddenly hushed.

He handed the painting to her, careful not to reveal too much of it. He had seen it, but he felt the need to allow her to experience this at her own pace. In somewhat of a private fashion.

He watched the older woman's face, watched as she placed her fingertips over the painting, her dark eyes filling with tears. "I can see," she said, her voice trembling, "I can see how much he loved me. It is there. Still."

"Who?" Gabriella asked.

"Bartolo. His name was Bartolo. An artist. And I…

I did not think there was any way I could sacrifice my position for love. But I'm old now, Gabriella. And I look at this and I see just how deep his feelings were. And then… Then we were thrown out of Isolo D'Oro, anyway. I asked myself every day what the sacrifice meant. I married a man who was suitable. I rejected the one who was not. For what? For a kingdom that crumbled. Seeing it again… Understanding… His love was more than I deserved. He did not deserve one so faithless as myself."

Gabriella's hands were folded in her lap and she was wringing them as though the queen's words were causing her great distress. "Grandmother, of course you did what you had to do. You did what you felt was right."

She sighed slowly, sadly. "It is all any of us can do, I'm afraid. But when your best isn't good enough it galls particularly with the sharp clarity of hindsight."

"I hate to cause you any further pain, Your Highness," Alex said. "But—"

"But your grandfather wants this painting returned to his possession," Lucia said, her tone grave.

"Yes. There are few things in his life that he prizes beyond money. Beyond anything. This painting is one of them. And though I can't tell you why, though it must seem strange as you are the subject of the painting, I can only tell you that it is an old man's greatest wish to have this again."

A tear rolled down her cheek, and Alex felt shamed by the emotional display for some reason. Shamed by how jaded he was, by how little credibility he gave to love and emotion when he saw such depth of it before him.

"Of course he can have it," Lucia said, her words shocking Alex down to the core.

"I will pay whatever you ask for it. He's prepared to compensate you handsomely."

She placed her hand over the painting again. "I don't want money. I *want* him to have it."

Alex met her gaze and nodded slowly. "He will."

Gabriella looked over at him, her expression filled with concern. "He isn't going to make a scandal with it?"

Alex shook his head. "No. My grandfather has no interest in scandal. He has no need for money."

Gabriella didn't ask if he was telling the truth. Something about that warmed his chest in a way that he wasn't certain he deserved.

"You must stay with us tonight, Alex," Lucia said.

His heart slammed against his breastbone. Denial was on the tip of his tongue. He shouldn't stay. He should go. But he was in no position to deny the older woman anything. "If you wish."

"And I do have a condition on giving you the painting."

Everything inside of him stilled. "Do you?"

The older woman nodded. "Gabriella shall go with you. She will help deliver the painting. Acting as an ambassador for our family."

"If you wish," he said again.

He had been desperate to escape Gabriella. Her tempting mouth, her soft touch. Nothing good could come of the attraction between them. Ever. Acting on it—more than they already had—was simply not an option. He would leave her untouched.

But in order for him to honor such a vow, he would need to get a good deal of distance between them.

This was not conducive to that goal.

He had honorable intentions, but he was a flesh and blood man. His spirit was willing but his flesh was very, very weak where she was concerned.

Still, he could not refuse.

"Of course," he said.

"Excellent," the queen said, "I will have some of the staff show you to your room. In the meantime, I would like to spend some time with my granddaughter."

Gabriella looked at the clock. It was nearly midnight, but she was still sitting awake in the library. Her conversation with her grandmother was playing over in her mind.

Lucia had been talking of an old love, of honor and duty perhaps not being everything. Of how her heart still ached, all these years later, when she looked at the painting.

It was so very strange for Gabriella, to hear her pragmatic grandmother speaking of love. They had spoken of it before, but always Lucia had been cautionary, because she had spoken of its loss.

Now, though...she said when she looked at that painting it made her feel so full. It made her realize all the beauty she had carried with her thanks to that ill-fated affair.

Made her realize she could never truly regret loving Bartolo, though she had not spent her life with him.

In addition to that, Gabriella's nerves were slightly frazzled with the idea of going to New York. More specifically, going with Alex.

It meant an extension on their time on Isolo D'Oro. More time just to be near each other. Circling around the larger things that neither of them were prepared to embrace.

She wanted it. She wanted more time with him. But she wasn't sure they should have it.

Things were… Well, they weren't normal between them. She had been looking forward to getting away from him, and now it appeared that wouldn't be happening. Of course, as much as she had been looking forward to there being some distance between them, she had also dreaded it.

The idea of going back to life as it had been before. As though she had never met him, as though they had never spent a week on Isolo D'Oro together. As though he had never called her beautiful, as though they had never kissed… The very idea of that was painful to her. Sat in her chest heavily like a leaden weight.

Which was probably the most telling sign that she didn't need to get away from him.

She stretched out on her tuffet, raising her arms, her hands balled into fists. She looked back down at the book she'd been reading and rubbed her eyes. It was a history book that focused on the art and culture of Isolo D'Oro. She had thought to look at it with her newfound real-life take on Isolo D'Oro to see if it might enhance it. Mainly, she had just sat there staring at the pages. Imagining the countryside. Being there, standing in the sunshine with Alex. Sitting in the garden with him, basked in moonlight as he tasted her. Touched her.

The door to the library opened and she startled.

Alex was standing there looking dashing, like a hero from a historical novel come to life.

He was wearing a white shirt open at the collar, the sleeves pushed up past his forearms. His hair looked as though he'd been running his fingers through it. He looked... Well, he looked like temptation personified.

"I thought I might find you here, Gabby," he said.

Her stomach did a little flip at his use of her nickname. "Yes, I do like the library."

She took her glasses off and rubbed at the bridge of her nose before putting them back in place.

"You look tired," he said.

"I am. But I couldn't sleep. I don't see how I could with everything that's happening tomorrow. New York. I've never been."

"I feel much the same."

"Why? Are you so anxious to get back to your real life?"

"No," he said, his tone dry. "That isn't the problem. It isn't fantasies about work that have me tossing and turning."

"If it isn't fantasies of work, then—" Her eyes clashed with his, the meaning of his words suddenly sinking in. "Oh."

"It would be better if you were not coming with me, Gabriella," he said, his tone full of warning.

She nodded slowly. "I have no doubt that's true."

"Doing what's right is incredibly tiresome," he said, walking deeper into the room, moving to sit in the chair across from hers. "And yet, it is the only thing that separates us from our parents, is it not?"

She nodded mutely.

"And I have to separate myself from them," he continued, his voice rough.

"You have," she said. "You're nothing like them at all."

"I have a half brother," he said, the words hitting her in a strange way, taking a moment for her to untangle. It seemed like a change of subject, and yet she knew it wasn't. Not really. "I found out about it when I was eleven years old. My father had an affair, as I told you before."

"My parents have had many," she said slowly.

"Affairs were nothing new," he continued as though she hadn't spoken. "But a child… My mother was incensed. He was humiliating her. Bringing shame upon her. Causing the world to believe she might not be desirable."

Gabriella tried to force a smile. "My mother screams a very similar refrain once every few months."

"This was different," Alex said. "I heard the altercation. It was Christmas. Snowing. Outside, the house had white lights strung all over it. As though they were trying to tell the world that we were normal. That we were a happy household. But inside… There were no lights. There was no tree. There was no happiness. And out there… My father's mistress brought her son. He was not much younger than I was. Ten, maybe. She stood out there screaming at my father, their son by her side. Telling him that he had to acknowledge him. My father refused. I…I looked out there and I saw him. And I knew exactly who he was. I told no one. My father drove off in a rage, my mother with him, as they tried to escape the scene. Tried to get away from his mistress. This monster of his own making. That was the night they were in the accident. It was the night they died. And the only people left alive who knew about Nate were his mother, himself and me. I told no one. I kept my half brother a secret."

"Oh, Alex, what a terrible burden."

"What a terrible burden I put on *him*. A child. But I was so angry, Gabby. I blamed him. He was what they were arguing about. And so… I chose comfort over truth. I chose to do what was easy, not what was right. Had I been any sort of man…"

"You weren't," she said, her chest tight. "You were a boy."

He shook his head, lowering it. "Not so much a boy." He looked younger when he said it. She felt like she could see him, as he'd been then. Young and trying so hard to be brave. To uphold the honor of his family in the only way he knew how.

"Yes," she said, her throat aching. "You were."

"He was entitled to that money. To come to the funeral of his father. To be acknowledged. I robbed him of that. Until we needed him. When my grandfather needed a bone marrow transplant I let everyone know about Nate's existence. He was Giovanni's only hope, you see. I…I cannot forgive myself for those things, Gabby. I cannot. They reveal that underneath everything I have tried to fashion for myself I am nothing more than my father's son. A man who uses people. A man who thinks nothing of putting others through hell in order to preserve his own comfort."

"That isn't true, Alex."

He curled his hand into a fist. "Yes, it is. There's a reason I'm telling you this."

"What's the reason?"

"Because I need you to understand. I need you to understand that I'm not a saint. That while I make a habit of practicing restraint, in the end I will only fail. In the end, I will reveal myself to be nothing more than what my blood has dictated I should be."

"We're more than blood, Alex, don't you think?"

"Are we?"

"You said yourself your grandfather took care of you. Your father is his son."

"In which case I have to ask myself if it was my mother. If some people are destined to drag down those who they love. Just another reason to stay away from me."

Her heart thundered, and she felt dizzy. He was so convinced he was toxic. And that was why they couldn't… She wasn't even entirely sure what they *couldn't*. Knew only that he was saying they couldn't, and she knew whatever it was that she wanted to. "But what about what I want?"

"You don't know what you want."

She blinked. "Of course I do. I'm a grown woman, Alessandro. You don't know what I want more than I do."

He got out of the chair, dropping to his knees so that he was down in front of her. He lifted his hand, brushing his thumb over her lower lip. He looked raw. Desperate. And she had to close her eyes, all of her focus going to that slow, sensual touch. "Gabriella, I have seen so much more of the world than you have. Believe me when I tell you that I know what you *should* want. What will keep you safe."

"No," she said, shaking her head.

"It cannot happen," he said, and she wasn't sure if he was telling her or himself. "I cannot kiss you again," he continued. "If I did, I would only sin greater."

She opened her eyes, looked down at him. At the creases on his forehead, the deep grooves that bracketed his face. Those lines made him all the more devastating. Without them, he would be too beautiful. But those lines—the evidence of years lived—gave him texture. Took him from mere beauty to devastating.

She ached. For him. With need for him. "All sins can be forgiven, can't they?"

"Not all, Gabby. My life—my childhood—is a testament to that. Some sins cause damage that is irreparable. That wound so deeply they will never heal. Ask my half brother about that. I would tell you to ask my parents, to ask my mother, but she's dead."

"But, Alex... If we both want each other..."

"You don't even know what it means to want, Gabriella."

Her chest felt tight, her eyes stinging with unshed

tears. “That isn’t fair, Alex, you don’t get to tell me that I don’t know what desire is when you’re the one who showed it to me. When you’re the one who made absolutely certain that I learned what it was.”

“I have already hurt you.” He shook his head, his tone filled with regret. “I would not like to do it again.”

“Then don’t.” She was on the verge of begging for something she had never imagined wanting with this much ferocity.

“I won’t.”

“Must you be so honorable? Must you choose this moment to be a man of your word? To be sincere?”

He nodded slowly. “If there is any moment where I must choose it, it is this one.”

She slid out of her chair, joining him on the floor. She took his hands in hers, leaning forward, touching her lips slightly to his. “But if you didn’t?” she asked, her mouth brushing his as she spoke the words.

He reached around behind her head, sifting his fingers through her hair and drawing her head back slightly, his dark eyes intent on hers. “If I did not, Gabby,” he said, his special nickname for her sending shivers along her spine. “If I didn’t, then I would lean in and I would kiss you, more deeply than you kissed me just now.”

“What else?” she asked, knowing she would burn for this. Past the point of caring.

“I would run my tongue along the line of your top lip before delving inside. I would taste you. So deep and long neither of us would be able to breathe. We wouldn’t want to breathe.”

She was shaking now, trembling with need. "Alex," she whispered.

"I would pull your T-shirt up over your head, so that I could see you," he said, resting his palm on her stomach, his touch scorching the material of her shirt. "So that I could feel how soft your skin is." He left his hand there, his other still buried deep in her hair. "Then I would remove your bra. Get a good look at those beautiful breasts. They are beautiful. *You* are beautiful. I have said it many times to you now, but I need you to understand how true it is. It is the deepest truth I know, Gabriella. Your beauty. As real as the night sky."

Tears filled her eyes and she made no move to wipe them away.

"I would trace your breasts with my tongue," he continued, "before moving down to kiss your stomach. Then I would strip off your pants, your underwear. For a moment I would just...look at you. I would be afraid to blink for fear that I would miss a moment of that beauty. I would taste you, tease you, touch you, until you were sobbing in my arms."

Gabriella closed her eyes, going still beneath his touch, focusing all of her attention on the pressure of his hand against her stomach, on the erotic words that were flowing from his mouth and over her like heated oil. "What then?" she asked.

"Oh, my darling, I would send you to the moon and back. I would make you scream with pleasure. Then, and only then, I would enter your body, slowly. I would be as careful with you as possible. But I fear it would not be as careful as I ought to be. Because by then...

then I would be desperate for you. Beyond thought. It is important that I make you scream before that, because I will not last long once I'm buried deep within you."

She let her lips fall open, her head drawn backward. "Yes," she said, the word a sigh.

"It would be heaven," he said, his voice a hoarse whisper. "To feel you all around me. You would be so tight, so hot and wet. For me. Only for me, Gabby. It would only be for me."

"Of course," she said. "It would only ever be for you, Alex."

She found herself swaying forward, her heart beating so quickly she thought she might faint.

Suddenly, Alex released his hold on her, standing up and putting as much distance between them as possible in one fluid movement. He was breathing hard, and she could see the press of his arousal against the front of his slacks. Could see that what he said was true. That he wanted her with a ferocity that he could not deny. That he would in fact love nothing more than to do everything he had just said.

And she wanted it. So badly that it echoed inside of her. An empty, aching need that only he could ever fill.

"We cannot, Gabby," he said.

"Why?" she asked, the word torture.

"Because I have committed so many grave sins already. I have hurt so many people. Gabriella, I will do nothing but hurt you. And it is the last thing on earth I want to do."

That was why she let him go. That was why she didn't press. Because of the desperation in his voice.

Because of how much he wanted to turn away from this. Because of how difficult it was for him. She would not add to his torture. Not after what she knew about him. Not after what he had told her about his parents, about his brother.

So she did nothing but nod slowly. Did nothing but watch him turn and walk out of the room all the while she sat there, shaking.

She felt cold suddenly. Where before she had only been hot.

She thought back to an earlier conversation they'd had as she sat there on the floor of her library, shivering. She had told him that one was much less likely to get scarred if they stayed in here. She almost laughed. Because she would never forget this. His words, his touch, was branded into her, a scar that would never heal. One that she had acquired—of all places—on the library floor.

It had been her place. The place she had always felt safe. Her refuge.

But it was his now. Irrevocably.

She was afraid it was the same for her.

CHAPTER TWELVE

GABRIELLA AVOIDED HIM for the entire plane ride. He supposed he couldn't blame her. He didn't know what he had been thinking. Confessing those things to her. Saying those words to a virgin.

To a woman that he could never touch. Not any more than he already had.

So, he had allowed her to avoid him. On the plane, then again in the car as she had stared out the window, gazing at the unfamiliar city skyline. And he had watched her reflection in the window, uncaring about the buildings that had become so familiar and mundane to him. New York City failed to enthrall him. What fascinated him was seeing them through her eyes. Wide and glistening as she took in everything around her, her mouth open slightly. Her lips looked so soft. He would give a good portion of his fortune to kiss them again.

He continued to think about her lips as they arrived at his penthouse in Manhattan. Normally, after this much time away from work he would go directly into his home office and set about catching up. But tonight… Tonight it simply didn't appeal.

The first thing he did when they arrived was set the painting up in the living room, taking a step back and looking at it for the first time since they had taken it from Isolo D'Oro.

"It's beautiful," Gabriella said, looking around the space, then at the painting. "All of this. I can't quite believe that I'm here."

"Yes," he said in agreement. But he didn't mean the view or his penthouse were beautiful. He meant her. Always her.

So then he looked at the painting to avoid looking at her. Close study of Gabriella's features could only lead to ruin. He had been so taken with the woman in the painting upon first viewing that he hadn't noticed much of the surrounding objects. For the first time he noticed that everything on the table of the vanity was painted in loving detail. That it was all very purposeful. The woman was wearing a necklace, the reflection of which could barely be seen in the mirror. Emeralds, and white diamonds. On her finger, almost entirely concealed by the tumbling locks of her dark hair, he could just make out the hint of a ring. There was a box, ornate and beautiful, certain to contain more jewelry. A tiara, set next to a beautiful bracelet. His breath caught, and he took a step closer. There was a book set on the vanity, as well.

That meant…

He moved closer still, scanning the surface of the table. Yes. There they were. A small pair of earrings.

"The Lost Mistresses," he said.

"What?" Gabriella asked.

"This is all of them. The artifacts my grandfather sent us after. They are all in this painting. The painting is the last one."

He turned to look at Gabriella. She was staring at him, her dark eyes wide. "What does that mean?"

"It means that I don't think you're being fanciful when you thought there might be a deeper link between our grandparents."

"But the painting… It was by someone called Bartolo."

"I know. But there is something. At one time your grandmother was in possession of every one of these objects. They were the dearest things to my grandfather's heart at another time."

"Alex…"

At that moment, Alex's phone rang. It was his half brother, Nate. Things were better between the two of them in recent years, but they had never been close. It surprised him that the other man would call him for anything.

"I have to get this."

Gabriella watched Alex as he paced out of the room, his phone pressed to his ear. It was strange to be here. In his house with him. Not domestic—because she doubted anything with Alex could ever feel domestic—but intimate. Of course, he hadn't stayed in the room with her to take his phone call. A stark reminder that they didn't really share much about their lives.

She looked back at the painting, looking closely this time at the objects in it. Alex's grandfather was

Giovanni Di Sione. As far as she knew he had no connection to the royal family. No connection to Isolo D'Oro. If not for this painting… On its own it was coincidental. Combined with these other objects…

Alex came back out of the room he had just gone into, his dark jacket on, his expression purposeful. "I have to go out. I will be back as soon as possible. You can help yourself to any of the food in the fridge. Or any of the alcohol."

"You don't have a library. What am I supposed to do?" She was only half teasing.

"You'll have to watch a movie, *cara mia*."

She did her best to keep busy while Alex was gone. But one hour turned into two, which turned into three. Then four. Before she knew it she was dozing on the couch, feeling rather sulky, and a little bit concerned. She should have asked him for his mobile number. So she could at least make sure he wasn't lying dead in an alley somewhere.

And once that thought was in her mind, she couldn't shake it.

Surely Alex was dead in an alley. Or if not dead, perilously close to bleeding out onto the cracked concrete sidewalk.

The idea made her stomach hurt. It was also ridiculous. Still, now that it had taken root, there it was.

She walked across the expansive living area and opened one of the bedroom doors to reveal a large bed with a black bedspread. She frowned. Not quite sure which room belonged to Alex. She opened the door next to it and saw another bed that looked almost exactly the same.

She let out an exasperated sigh and walked deeper into that room, letting her fingertips trail over the lush bedding. She was tired. She hadn't unpacked any of her things since she wasn't sure which room she would be staying in. She had changed into her sweats to get a bit more comfortable but she wasn't going to go hunting for her pajamas.

She sat on the edge of the bed, bouncing slightly on the mattress before lying back. She looked over at the clock, the glowing blue numbers showing that it was well after midnight.

She suddenly had a thought that was even more disturbing than the idea of Alex dying in an alley. Maybe he was out with a woman. Why else would he stay out all night? If the issue wasn't that he couldn't make it home, then he wasn't here because he didn't *want* to be home.

The only reason she could think that a man would want to stay out all night was if he was with a woman.

He might be doing the things with her that he wouldn't do with Gabriella. Acting out those words he'd said to her, so deeply erotic. As if he'd woven a fantasy together that was spun with a desire called up from the very depths of her soul. Desire not even she had realized she possessed.

She hated whoever the other woman was. A woman who would—even for a night—capture *all* of Alex's attention. Not just a piece of him.

Not just his smile, or the glint in his eye. Not just his rough, perfect voice, or promises he could never keep. But his body. No barriers between them.

She would touch him everywhere, this mystery woman. Her hands beneath his clothes, learning secrets about him Gabriella would never, ever know.

She burned. She didn't know that jealousy would burn from the inside out. Scalding her. Making her feel raw and restless and angry. She had never been jealous before.

There had never been a man before.

She had been too busy burying herself in dusty books. Wrapping herself in a blanket of safety, insulated by the shelves of her library. By the family estate.

Protecting herself from more rejection.

What she'd said to him had been true. Her own parents didn't truly want her. Didn't really choose her. It was difficult to believe that anyone else would. She was invisible. That was the best case scenario. The worst was that she was in the way.

She swallowed hard, closing her eyes tight and curling her knees up to her chest.

The next thing she knew, she heard heavy footsteps coming into the room. Her eyes snapped open, locking onto the clock. It was after three now.

She was on her back, moving into a sitting position. "Alex?" she asked, her heart thundering heavily.

"Gabriella?" Her name sounded strange on his lips. As though he were convinced she was some sort of apparition.

"Yes. Is this your room? I should have investigated

further, but I..." *Didn't want to.* She couldn't very well finish that sentence.

Couldn't tell him that a part of her had been hoping this was his room. That she would encounter him later.

Shortsighted. As well as a little bit creepy. Shortsighted mainly because she was still wearing her sweats, which was hardly the official uniform of seduction.

"You were asleep," he said.

"Yes. I fell asleep waiting for you to come back. I thought maybe you were dead." Her other concern hit her, cold and hard. Obviously he wasn't dead, but he could very well still have been having sex. "Were you with a woman?"

He let out a heavy sigh and sat down on the edge of the bed. "No. Would it have bothered you if I was?"

"That's a stupid question. Of course it would have." She saw no point in playing coy. She was sleepy, and cranky, and a little bit gritty behind the eyelids. She was in no state to play coy.

He shifted his position, lying down beside her, and her breath caught. There was still a healthy expanse of mattress between them, but still. "It was my brother. My half brother, Nate. I told you about Nate."

"Yes, you did."

"He found the ring. It has an inscription on it. *B.A.*"

"Bartolo," she said.

"Probably. They are the same initials on the painting, Gabriella. They were his. *She* was his, just like your grandmother said. But it's more than that. I know that my grandfather had to start over when he came to

America. And I wonder just how completely the new beginning was."

"You think he was my grandmother's lover." His suspicions mirrored her own. It made sense. There just didn't seem to be another way someone could possess all of the same objects that appeared in the painting. More than that, it was her grandmother's reaction to everything. The fact that she had seemed to want Giovanni to have the painting. "She knows," Gabriella said. "She figured it out before we did."

She thought back to the way that her grandmother had looked at Alex when he'd first come into the room at the estate in Aceena. "I bet you look like him," she said. She couldn't see him now; she was staring through the darkness, looking in his direction, barely able to make out his silhouette against the dark bedspread. "I mean, like he did."

"I guess that's why she let me take it in the end."

"They loved each other. They couldn't be together because she had to marry royalty. My grandfather." Suddenly, her throat felt tight, painful. "The artist… Bartolo…he did love her very much. I know. You can see it. It must've killed him to part with those things."

"Not quite. He's still very much alive. For now. It wounded him to part with them. I wonder if he thinks seeing them will return some of his strengths."

"It isn't the objects he needs," she said, her voice wistful.

"You are right." He reached across the distance between them, drawing his fingertips slowly across her cheek. She closed her eyes, tried to fight the tears that were welling in them.

"It is a tragedy, Alex. To think of that. Just think of how much they loved each other all those years..."

She could see her life suddenly, stretching before her. Bleak and lonely. She realized that she could never marry a man who didn't incite fantasy in her. Down to her very core. That she couldn't possibly ever marry a man who understood art the way she did, or appreciated books, or had a library. That she couldn't marry a man who was closer to her age and experience or didn't think of her as an owl. Because that man wouldn't be Alex.

It was Alex for her. Now and always. Forever.

She realized now that maybe she had not been protecting herself so much as waiting for this. For him. For the kind of desire that reached down deep and took over your soul. For the kind of desire that went well beyond common sense. The kind that didn't care if heartbreak lay down the road. Even if it was a short distance away.

She thought of the way her grandmother had spoken of Giovanni—because she was certain that Giovanni and Bartolo were one and the same—of the fact that no matter the heartbreak she could never regret their time together, and it made her tremble. She wasn't certain if she was that strong. To grab hold of an experience while giving no thought to the pain that the consequences might cause.

It was the kind of thing she had been avoiding all of her life. Being like her parents.

But they don't do anything because of love. It's because of selfishness.

Her chest felt like it had cracked open. Of course. That was the difference. Action was always empty, dry, when there was no love. There had been a time when her mother had kissed her good-night before going off to a party, but the gesture had been empty. And the proof was in the fact that now that Gabriella was an adult neither of her parents ever spoke to her. Those goodnight kisses could not be a happy memory, not now that she could see them so clearly for what they were. The proper motions that her parents went through in order to salve what little conscience they had.

This…this had nothing to do with going through the motions. Had nothing to do with doing the right thing. It was just…need.

Alex was a man so far removed from the world. Everything in it seemed to move around him. And he seemed to exist in it untouched.

She wanted to touch him. Not just his skin, but beneath it. She wanted to reach him down deep where his heart beat. Wanted to heat him from the inside out, warm his blood, his soul.

Mostly, she just wanted everything he had promised her back in the library. When they parted, the wound would linger. No matter what happened now. If he was going to leave a scar, she wanted it to be such a scar. So deep, so affecting, it would never heal.

She inched toward him, reaching out and placing her hand over his cheek, mirroring his action.

"Gabriella," he said, his voice a growl, warning.

She didn't listen to it.

She leaned forward, claiming his mouth with hers, kissing him as though she had a right to do it. As though she knew how.

She knew that he would recognize her limited technique, because she had learned it from him. It was all she knew. So when she traced the seam of his lips with her tongue, she was keenly aware of the fact that she was plagiarizing his earlier kiss. But if he was aware of it, he didn't show it. He was still beneath her touch, completely motionless. But he hadn't pushed her away.

They parted, her hand still resting on his cheek. She could hear ragged breathing filling the space between them, but couldn't tell if it was his or hers. Both.

"Gabriella," he said again, "you have no idea what you're asking for. No idea what you're doing."

She pressed her forehead to his, the tips of their noses touching. "I want to make love. I know what that is, Alex. Sex. I've never wanted it before. Not in a specific sense. But I do now."

"I can't offer you anything. I won't make you any promises, because I will only break them."

"Maybe."

"Certainly."

"Well, tomorrow the sky could fall, or I could get hit by a bus—"

"It won't, and you won't."

"You don't know that. We don't know anything beyond right now. I saw my grandmother's face. I know there was a lot that she regretted. But I don't think she ever regretted being with Bartolo." She knew that these words were tantamount to admitting that she felt more for him than simple attraction, but she couldn't bring herself to care.

"I am the worst of sinners. I condemned my half brother to a life lived outside of the family. It was me who stood in his way. Made him feel like he could never be close to us. He told me that tonight. It is on me, Gabriella."

"Alex—"

"I carry the blood of my father. Weak selfishness that I've worked a very long time to overcome. So believe me when I tell you I will regret nothing of what happened here tonight. My nobility is nothing more than a construct. There is no conviction behind it. But you, Gabriella, you, I fear will regret this."

"Maybe. Tomorrow. But not now. And the only thing we have for sure is now."

A feral sound rumbled low in his chest and he shifted positions so that he was over her, his arms braced on either side of her shoulders.

She locked her leg over the back of his calf, an action designed to hold him prisoner even though she knew it wouldn't be truly effective. Still, she wanted him to know that she wanted him here. Desperately.

"Alex," she said, his name a prayer on her lips. She bracketed his face with her hands, looking at him, trying to see what he was thinking, even through the darkness. "Don't you know how much I want you?"

He tensed, pulling away from her slightly. Her heart hammered hard in her chest, clawing at her like a small beast.

"Alex," she said his name again, ready to beg him if she needed to.

He flicked on the light. The way it illuminated his face cast the hollows of his cheekbones into darkness, adding a tortured quality to his features.

"If I'm going to sin, then I'm going to do it with my eyes open," he said. "If I'm going to have you, then I'm going to look at you while I do it."

She breathed a sigh of relief, sliding her hands around to the back of his neck, holding him to her. "I'm glad."

"You won't be. Gabriella, I am too old for you, too jaded, too tired. I can offer you nothing. It's a strange thing to realize that. I am a billionaire. I have more money than I could ever spend in a lifetime. I have all of these things. And for a great many years that has been good enough. I have had whoever I wanted in my life when I wanted them. I have had ultimate control over my own reputation. Wielding it like a sword when I needed to. But none of that helps me here. None of that helps with you. It is…insufficient, and I am a man who is not used to falling short."

"You have yourself. That's all I have to offer. That has to be enough."

"Tonight it will be."

Alex lowered his head, kissing her deeper, harder, than he had before. A restless groove in the pit of her stomach spread through her entire body. Like a creeping vine that took over everything in its path. Winding itself around her limbs, around her throat, making it impossible for her to breathe. Binding her to Alex in a way that was so intense, so permanent, she knew that parting from him would be so much more painful than she'd imagined it would be.

But she wouldn't stop. Even knowing that, she wouldn't stop.

This time, he did not keep his hands still. He did not simply press his palm to her stomach. He let himself explore her body, his fingertips skimming her breasts before he took one firmly in hand, sliding his thumb over one hardened nipple. She gasped, arching against him, her entire body alive with sensation.

"This is a gift I don't deserve," he said, his tone fractured and reverent.

She couldn't speak, but if she could, she would have told him that she was the one receiving a gift. So many lonely, isolated years. So much hollowness inside of her. She had hidden herself away to avoid being hurt again. To avoid more rejection. The neglect of her parents had been enough. And when she went out, she put on a mask. She didn't let anyone see both parts of herself. Princess Gabriella never messed with Gabriella as she was day to day. She didn't give anyone the chance to reject who she really was. But Alex had it all. Held it all in the palm of his hand as surely as he held her body. And he was here. He was touching her. Pouring out all of this attention, all of this care, onto her.

It was so beautiful she could barely breathe.

He pushed her shirt up over her head, baring her breasts to him. She had taken her bra off when she had put her sweats on, and now she was relieved. One less barrier between the two of them. She didn't want anything standing between them. Didn't want any walls up whatsoever. She wanted to give him everything—her body, her soul—and no matter how foolish she knew it was, she couldn't stop that desire that roared through her like an untamed animal.

It would end in heartbreak. It would end in destruction.

But when she was old, she would look back and she would have this moment. She would have Alex. And she knew without a doubt that giving in to pure, true love was something she would never regret.

She had no idea how this moment had happened. How this woman in this bed, in this man's arms, was the same woman she had been only a week ago.

She was changed. She was new. Already, he had changed the world for her. Lifted the veil so that she could see the colors more clearly, feel pleasure more keenly, feel desire sharp like a knife's blade sliding over her skin.

It was painful, incandescent and magical all at once.

He made quick work of her sweatpants and underwear, leaving her completely bare to him, his dark gaze filled with hunger, a desire that couldn't be denied, as he took in the sight of her body.

"Gabby," he said, her name a whispered prayer. "I never thought I appreciated art. But this… You. You are every bit of beauty a painter has ever tried to capture onto canvas. The fields, the mountains, all of the smooth female skin that has ever been painted in an attempt to show some of the glory that is here on this earth. They fall short. It all falls short of you."

Her heart felt so full she thought it might burst. How was this real? How was this man saying these things to her?

It was inconceivable that she might be enough for this man.

That he was afraid that he might not be enough for her. That he was apologizing for the lack of what he had to give.

It didn't make sense. It didn't make sense at all.

But she reveled in it. Accepted it. Took it as her due for so many years of feeling like she was less than.

"I need to see you," she said, her voice a hoarse whisper she barely recognized.

"Not yet," he said. "Not yet."

He lowered his head, kissing her neck, kissing a trail along her collarbone, and down to the swell of her breasts. Then he shifted, taking her nipple into his mouth, sucking it in deep before tracing it with the tip of his tongue. The pleasure that sparked along her veins was shocking, white-hot and almost terrifying in its intensity. There was so much more to making love than a simple caress, and still, this had nearly burned her to the ground. How would she survive at all?

She wouldn't. Not the same.

Nothing passed through the fire and came out the same. But at this point, she didn't want to. She wanted to be changed. By him. Irrevocably, eternally.

He continued his exploration, peppering kisses over her stomach, encircling her belly button with the soft stroke of his tongue before traveling downward. "You see, *cara mia*, were I to take my clothes off, I would not be able to resist sinking inside of you. And you deserve more than that. You deserve for me to take my time. As I told you in the library, once I'm very deep within you I will not be able to hold myself back. And so, your pleasure must come first. Now."

He gripped her hips, drawing her toward his mouth, her thighs spread wide as he pressed his lips to the center of her need. A short, shocked scream escaped her mouth as he lavished attention on that sensitive bundle of nerves with his tongue, as he tasted her, slowly, deeply. He shifted again, pressing his finger against the entrance of her body as he continued to lavish pleasure on her with his mouth. The invasion was foreign, but it felt good.

He added a second finger, stretching her slightly this time, the vague painful sensation drawing her out of her reverie, but only for a moment.

Before long she grew accustomed to that, pleasure mounting inside of her again as he established a steady rhythm, working his hands and tongue in time with each other. She felt need, tension, gathering in the pit of her stomach like a ball of electricity, scattering outward, sending shocks along her system as it continued to build an intensity. So hot, so bright, she felt like she might burst with it.

And it did burst. Rolling over her in waves unending, unfathomable in its depth. She gripped the bed covers, trying to use something to root her to the earth, anything. Because without it, she feared that she would lose hold of herself entirely.

He rose up above her, kissing her deeply, her own

desire a musky flavor on his tongue. "Are you all right?" he asked, his chest rising and falling with the effort it took for him to breathe.

"Yes. More than all right. I'm… Alex, I didn't know it was like this."

"What did you think it would be?" His words slurred as though he were drunk.

"I didn't know. Because I didn't know it would be you."

"Does it matter *so* much that it's me?" She sensed a rawness behind that question, a vulnerability.

"That's the only thing that matters."

He growled, kissing her again as she grabbed hold of the edge of his button-up shirt, undoing the buttons as quickly as possible. She spread her hands over that broad expanse of chest. His hard muscles…that perfect sprinkling of chest hair that reminded her just how much of a man he was. How different they were. It was heaven to touch him like this. To finally have the promise of that glorious body fulfilled, in her hands. She pushed the shirt from his shoulders and threw it over the side of the bed, running her hands down his back, exploring the intricate musculature there. She parted her thighs, arching against him, feeling the evidence of his arousal against where she was wet and aching for him already. She should be satisfied, after what he had just done for her. She found she was far from it.

"I need you. How can I need you this badly after all of that?" she asked, her voice trembling.

"I would tell you that's sex, *cara.* I would tell you that's desire. But it is not sex or desire in any way that

I know it. I do not shake for want of being inside of a woman. You make me shake. You make me feel as though I won't be able to breathe until I have you. Until I'm joined to you. What witchcraft is that, Gabriella? You must tell me."

"How can I? I'm just a virgin. You are supposed to be wise. You're supposed to be the one teaching me."

"How can I? When I feel you have so much to teach me." He kissed her gently as his hands moved to his belt. She could hear him undoing the buckle slowly and a shiver of anticipation ran through her. She helped him push his pants and underwear down his narrow hips and he sent them over the side of the bed to join the rest of their clothes. She could feel him, feel his hot hard length, pressed against her heat.

"I want to see you," she said, her voice husky, unrecognizable to her own ears. "I've never seen a naked man before."

He straightened, a dull slash of red coloring his cheekbones. "So many honors I don't deserve, Princess."

He sounded tortured, and at any other time she might have felt sorry for him, or wondered why. But not now. How could she feel sorry for him when she was too busy exulting in this triumph for herself?

He was perfect. Masculine beauty depicted in sculpture could never have prepared her for Alex.

Marble was cold, lifeless. It might show the shape of a man, but it didn't show the vitality. His life, his strength. It was everything and more. His broad shoulders, perfectly defined chest and washboard stomach, bisected by a line of hair that ran down to his very evident desire was enough to take a breath away.

He was so very…large. Thick. Part of her was made nervous by that, the other part marveled at the glory that was in front of her. The glory that would be hers.

"You're right," she said, her words hushed.

"About what?"

"You are in possession of very rampant masculinity."

He laughed, the sound tortured. "I only hope that it isn't too rampant for you."

"It's just perfect for me. How can it be anything else?"

He dropped forward on his knees, between her thighs, his hands on her shoulders. She looked up at him, her heart pounding heavily.

"You're beautiful," she said.

"And you are more than I deserve," he said, kissing her, wrapping his arm around her waist and drawing her body hard up against his as he pressed the head of his arousal against the entrance to her body.

She winced slightly, bracing herself for his invasion. It hurt. But she wanted it. There was no question. Even as he pressed forward, and she stretched around him, trembling as he joined their bodies together, she didn't want anything else but this. It was desire so perfectly and beautifully realized, the fulfillment of fantasy. Not because it brought pleasure. But because she was joined to him. Because they were one. Even though it hurt.

And when he thrust deep within, completing their

joining, there was no pleasure to be found at all. Not in the physical sense.

But her soul felt alive. Complete. For the first time.

And as the pain slowly began to fade and the pleasure began to build again, she felt so full with it that she could scarcely breathe.

Desire was a wild, needy thing inside of her. She wanted it to be satisfied. Needed it to be satisfied. And yet at the same time she wanted this to go on forever. Wanted to prolong the moment where she would reach her peak. Because once that happened it was the end. Of this perfect moment where they were joined. Connected. Where they were one with each other. The desire to cling to him, to cling to this, was doing battle with the desire to find completion. Ferocious, intense. She didn't know which one would win. Didn't know which one she wanted to win.

"Gabby," he said her name. Just her name.

Gabby would always belong to him. Only to him. The very idea of someone else saying it made her ill.

His teeth scraped the edge of her collarbone, the small slice of pain mingling with the pleasure, drawing her back to earth, making her feel so acutely aware of everything. So perfectly in tune with her body, and his.

She could feel his building pleasure along with hers. Could feel how close to the edge he was as his muscles tensed, as his control frayed.

She opened her eyes, determined to watch his face. Determined to watch this man who was everything she was not. Hardened, masculine beauty. Experienced. World-weary. She would watch him as he felt the same thing she did. As they experienced this storm of pleasure on the same level. It reduced them, this desperation, reduced them down to their souls. To ravenous, needy things that had nothing beyond this moment, this common need.

It was how Princess Gabriella D'Oro, recent virgin and definite bookworm, met with Alessandro Di Sione, rumored fearsome monster and a man who claimed to have a hardened heart. How they not only met, but understood each other. Spoke in perfect words that each other alone could understand. How had she ever thought they were different? How had she ever looked at him and seen a gulf they couldn't bridge? They had. She was closer to him now, in this moment, than she had ever been to another person in her life.

It was powerful, fearsome, awe-inspiring. These needs that only the other could meet. That only the other could inspire. A hunger only he could arouse and satisfy.

"Alex," she said, arching against him, the source of her pleasure meeting his heart and body as he thrust deep within her. A shower of sparks rained over her, pleasure breaking over her like an electrical storm, flashes of light blinding brilliance behind her eyes. She closed them, but only for a moment. Then she forced them open again, watched his face as he, too, gave himself over to this thing between them. She watched as that face, that face that could have been carved from granite, softened, the lines on his forehead shifting, a look of pure pain and desperation contorting his features as he growled his release, his entire body trembling as he spilled himself deep inside of her. She held him, as pleasure continued to rack his frame, as aftershocks kept moving through her in an endless wave.

They were connected in this. This pleasure. This moment.

And when it was over they simply lay there, entwined in each other. Breathing together.

She knew that Alex would feel regret later. Because no matter what he said he wasn't a monster. She had to wonder why he was so desperate to convince not only others, but himself, of the fact that he was.

She knew it came down to his fear that he would become like his father. She knew enough about him to understand that. But she also knew him well enough to understand it would never be him.

He had made some mistakes in his life with his family, but he had been a young man. Barely more than a boy. She had made far fewer mistakes. If only because she interacted with less people. Life wasn't as difficult when you hid from it.

He looked at himself and saw nothing but a potential monster and he was dedicated to forcing others to see the same.

She knew better.

He was so dry. So funny and brilliant. He cared. Very deeply. For her, for everyone else around him. He pretended he didn't. The way he looked after his grandfather, the pain that laced his voice when he spoke of his half brother and his past treatment of him, the way he had taken such great care with her, told an entirely different story than the narrative Alex had spent so many years carefully constructing.

He had only given when she had pushed. And both passed the point of resistance. He had never pressured her for anything, and she knew without a doubt that he never would have.

He was a hero in her eyes and yet he insisted on casting himself as the villain.

She wished, more than anything, that he could see himself through her eyes. That he could see himself clearly. She would make it her mission to change his thoughts on himself. She would.

No, it wouldn't change in a moment. No matter how much she might want to. She was going to have to show him, over time. Show him the man he really was. But in order to do that she would have to stay with him. Leave Aceena. Convince him to attempt to make some kind of relationship with her. He had arrangements with women, he had said as much. Why couldn't he have one with her?

Eventually…he would have to see that they were good together. Her thoughts were spinning, her entire body humming. There was so much going on in her brain. But she had never been good at letting things rest. She was always trying to solve the problem. Always trying to get down to the truth. To figure out the source of the problem so that she could stamp it out.

Unfortunately, there was no history book she could look at to conduct a simple study on Alex.

She would have to study him in person. Not a hardship, really.

"You're very quiet," he said.

"Thinking," she said honestly.

"About?"

She bit her lip. She could hardly tell him that she was plotting ways to convince him to love not only her, but himself.

"You're very good in bed," she said, rather than telling him the exact thoughts that were on her mind. That was what her body was thinking about, anyway. "Granted, I have no one else to compare to, but I can't imagine there are very many men who exceed your skill."

"It isn't about skill, Gabby." He brushed her hair out of her face, his body still entwined with hers. "This is chemistry."

A burst of warmth fired up in her heart, then fizzled out just as quickly. It was more than that. For her, it was so much more than that.

She would show him. She would find a way. After a lifetime spent hiding away she knew one thing for certain. After standing in the light with Alex, she would never retreat back into the shadows.

CHAPTER THIRTEEN

ALEX HAD CALLED himself ten kinds of villain since that first night he had taken Gabriella to bed. Of course, it had not stopped him from taking her to bed every night since. She was everything he had fantasized she might be. Beautiful, soft. And her enjoyment of study had come into play in some erotic and interesting ways he had not imagined. She was very thorough.

She had explored his body as though he were an ancient text she was attempting to pull meaning from.

No one had looked that deeply into him and his secrets in…ever. He was stone people built legend around. But no one ever looked beneath to see the man. And he'd kept it that way. For a reason. Several reasons.

He found it hard to keep Gabby at that same distance. Found it hard to even want to keep her at a distance.

She was soft and beautiful, and more generous than she should be. And he spent late nights not only exploring her body, but lying next to her, skimming his hands over her bare curves while she read passages from favorite books to him, and did her very best to educate him about art and other things he didn't care about in the least.

But he liked hearing the words on her lips. Enjoyed the way they poured over him like warm honey, soothing him in a soul-deep way he hadn't imagined possible. Mostly because it was easy to imagine he didn't have a soul.

Because a man who had kept his own half brother a secret, who shared the blood of the most selfish, pleasure-seeking bastard on earth, could hardly have regular human emotions. Could hardly feel softness, tenderness, for a beautiful woman he had nothing in common with.

Could hardly be soothed to a soul he didn't have.

But with Gabby things felt different. Possible. Ridiculous, since he was a billionaire and *everything* was possible. He could have small mammals on jet packs delivered by noon if he wanted. One princess shouldn't make anything feel more possible.

Still, it was the word that came to mind, whether it made sense or not. Well, there were other words, but none of them were appropriate.

He hadn't ever cared about anything like that before, but with her he did. He couldn't afford to care, and he needed to get back to work. But until he dealt with his grandfather, the painting and his family, he couldn't.

Fortunately, they were meeting today. Gabriella would come with him; she would be part of passing the painting to his grandfather, as her grandmother had asked. And then she would go home.

The thought shouldn't make it feel like a knife's blade had been slipped beneath his skin and twisted.

"Hi, Alex," she said, coming out of his bedroom right then, dressed in nothing but a T-shirt. His T-shirt. And what would have been cliché on another woman was new on her. As though he'd never before seen it. As though no woman had ever slipped her lover's T-shirt on over her luscious curves after an evening of passion.

Gabby was an original no matter what she did. Perhaps because she was his, and only his. Because no other man had touched her, no other man had kissed her. He'd never been with a virgin before. Maybe he was just archaic enough for it to matter.

He hadn't thought he was. But then, he hadn't thought he had a soul, either.

"Good morning, Gabriella," he said, lifting his coffee mug to his lips.

"So, we meet with your family today?" she asked, her dark eyes liquid, hopeful for some reason. Perhaps she was ready to be rid of him. Ready to go back to Aceena.

But last night she had not sounded like a woman ready to be rid of him.

"Yes. Soon. You'll have to get dressed in something other than that."

She smiled, and it was a little bit wicked. On that innocent mouth that he had trained to do such sensual things, it was another Gabby original. "You mean I can't wear this to go and meet your family?"

The way she said those words. Meeting his family. They did something to him. Grabbed hold of something down deep inside of him and twisted hard. He was torn between an intense longing and a fierce need to reject the desire.

He cleared his throat. "It would probably be best if you are wearing pants of some kind when I introduce you to my grandfather."

"Because I would shock him?" She seemed rather pleased by the thought.

"Because he would steal you away from me."

"No one could do that, Alex," she said, crossing the distance between them and kissing him on the cheek. "But I will get dressed."

She turned and walked back out of the room and he was left wondering what the hell had just happened here. What was happening in his life? Gabriella seemed to be happening. And far from being the harmless little bookworm she had seemed to be when he first met her at the door of the estate in Aceena, it appeared now that she was a rather intense bespectacled whirlwind.

Today all of the Lost Mistresses would be reunited again, would be with his grandfather. He had helped make his grandfather's last wish come true. He would focus on that. What happened beyond today? Well, what happened beyond today would be what was necessary. Gabriella returning home was necessary. Gabriella getting as far away from him as possible before he did even more damage was necessary.

Damage was all he would do. It was all he was capable of. She would only need to ask Nate to know that was true. Would only need to ask every other woman who had ever passed through his life. Every one of his siblings he had been distant with, emotionally unavailable to.

The idea of Gabriella returning home should fill him with nothing more than a sense of completion. He could get back to his real life. Get back to the running of his company, could forget treasure hunts for lost paintings and art lessons and owlish eyes.

Instead, he felt as though his chest was full of lead.

But he had spent the past thirty-six years ignoring his feelings. He saw no reason to start engaging with them now.

He didn't often make his way to the Di Sione family estate. As far as he was concerned it held nothing but ghosts from his past. Too many memories of what it was like to be a lonely little boy who just lost his parents. An angry, fearful eleven-year-old who had hidden the existence of a half brother to protect a man who didn't deserve protecting.

He shook off the thought as he walked through the grand entry, determined to shed every last one of his memories and feelings like mud on his boots with each step he took.

He could hear Gabriella following behind him, her footsteps timid on the marble as she did so. He was carrying the painting, making his way into the family sitting room, scarcely feeling prepared to face not only his grandfather, but his assorted siblings.

When he walked in, every eye in the room landed on him, the painting he was carrying and the woman who was trailing behind him. He couldn't remember the last time they'd all stood in one room.

Hell, Dario and Dante were standing beside each other. The identical Di Siones finally speaking again after years of discord.

Everyone gathered here in this room, united in this mission for Giovanni. This would have been impossible before. Before the quest Alex had been so quick to mock.

Nate, who he had always had the most challenging relationship with, was here, too, with his pregnant lover. And when Alex looked at him…he didn't feel the weight of his failure, of his guilt. Not anymore.

Now he wondered. Wondered if it had ever truly been about these artifacts, or if they had been searching for a different kind of treasure all along.

"What's the matter with all of you?" he asked, his tone sardonic. "Have you never seen a painting before? Or a woman?"

Giovanni stayed seated, his dark eyes trained on Gabriella. And Alex knew that his grandfather was seeing the same spark of resemblance in Gabby as Lucia had seen in him.

"It has been a very long time since I have seen such a painting," his grandfather said slowly. "Or," he continued, looking at Gabby, "such a woman."

Gabriella looked up at him, her eyes searching. All of this was confirming what they both already suspected, but Alex was eager to hear the story from his grandfather's own lips. "There is not only a woman in this painting," Alex said. "The mistresses are here, as well." He turned, standing the painting up on the mantel.

His siblings were no longer looking at him, but at the painting.

"I sense there is a story here, *Nonno*," Alex said, his voice hushed. "And I can't imagine you sent all of us on a worldwide scavenger hunt only to keep the truth hidden from us forever."

Giovanni rubbed his chin, his expression thoughtful. "You are right there, Alessandro. I had no intention of keeping you in the dark forever. Nearly a century is long enough for a man like me, to live, to hold on to his secrets."

"Well, I expect you to live a few more years," Alex said, knowing that such a thing was highly unlikely, but hoping to speak it into existence, anyway.

"From your lips to God's ears," Giovanni said. "But in the event the Man upstairs is busy, too busy to hear such a pronouncement, I suppose I should speak my piece now. You may have begun to suspect that Giovanni Di Sione is not my given name. I was born Bartolo Agosti."

"The letters *BALDO* on the jewelry..." Dario said.

Giovanni smiled.

"The inscription on the pieces I gave to Lucia... Bartolo Agosti, Lucia D'Oro. When I came to America I reinvented more than simply my fortune. I did not just recreate my wealth, I recreated my legend. I was born on Isolo D'Oro. The son of a wealthy family. My brother and I often played with a little girl in the gardens of the palace. It was a simple time on the island.

The royal family was in no danger and they moved about freely, mixing with those who were beneath them, playing in the sunshine. I was one such child who was far beneath the princess, though I was titled. I still wasn't a prince—never destined to be a king.

"My friendship with that little girl became much more. As we grew, so did our feelings. But sadly for Lucia and myself, while spending a few amusing hours in the garden together was acceptable, it would not make for an acceptable marriage. I knew that things between the two of us had to come to an end. I knew that she had to take up the mantle of her destiny, not take up a life with a man such as myself. But before we parted, I wanted to paint her. I wanted to paint her with the gifts that I had given to her—tokens of our affection. I wanted to show her that no matter what I said, no matter how things ended, I wanted her to be able to look at this painting and see how I loved her.

"But in the end, when I told her we could not be, when I told her she had to marry the man her parents had selected for her, she was angry. She gave everything back. All of the gifts. Including the painting. I kept them, the only pieces of my Lucia that I retained. I kept them until I was forced to part with them. Part with them or starve. But the painting…I sent it back to her. I never knew what she did with it. I never heard from her. Never found out if her husband intercepted it, if her family kept it from her. But I wanted her to look at it again. With distance between us, with years between that heartbreak, I wanted her to look at it and understand that what I did was not because I cared so little for her. But because I cared so very much."

He turned his focus to Gabriella.

"Tell me, my dear. Did your grandmother have the painting?"

Gabriella's expression was so soft, so caring, her dark eyes nearly liquid. "She did. When the family was banished from Isolo D'Oro she had to leave it. But she hid it. She held on to it. She knew just where it was, and when she saw it..."

"She saw it again?"

"Yes. Before we came here to New York. We returned to Aceena and showed it to her. It was her one request. She wanted you to have it back, but she wanted to see it first. She cares, Bartolo," Gabriella said, using Alex's grandfather's real name, a name he had doubtless not heard for years. "She cares so very much."

"And that, right there, is a gift that supersedes all of this."

"That's nice, Grandfather. So you send us on a field trip around the world to find your trinkets and all you needed was emotional reassurance the whole time," Dario said, his tone dry. "If I had known that, I might have simply purchased you a nice card."

"God knows you needed a diversion, Dario. I also reunited you with the mother of your child and the love of your life." His grandfather snorted. "You could perhaps say thank you."

"I could." But he didn't.

He did, however, step back and take hold of Anais's hand, stroking his thumb over her knuckles.

That was, for Dario, as much of a sincere gesture as would likely be demonstrated.

"It's strange," Giovanni said, "but I expected a greater sense of completion. Upon seeing everything together I thought perhaps I would feel a sense of resolution. But they are simply things."

"Perhaps you were waiting for a person. Not an object."

Everyone turned toward the sound of the thin, elderly voice coming from the doorway of the sitting area. It was Gabriella's grandmother, Lucia. The older woman was slightly stooped, but still, her bearing was regal. She was dressed in a deep purple that complemented her olive skin and dark eyes. And though her hair was white, though her skin was aged, it was undeniable that she was the woman in the picture. Not so much because of the resemblance she bore, but because the love that shone from Giovanni's eyes matched the passion in the artist's brushstrokes.

Giovanni stood, the move slow, labored. It was clear that he stood on unsteady legs, but in spite of the difficulty, he began to cross the room, closing the distance between himself and his long-lost love.

"I have a feeling we could have saved ourselves a lot of work if we had simply gone and fetched her in the first place," Dario said.

But they regarded each other cautiously, and then Lucia stretched out her hand and curled her fingers around Giovanni's, squeezing them gently. "Bartolo," she said, her voice thick with tears.

"It has been too long."

To everyone's surprise, Lucia laughed. "I would say an excess of fifty years is most definitely too long to be parted from the love of your life."

"I hope very much that there was love in your last fifty years regardless," Giovanni said.

Lucia nodded slowly. "There was. There is. But that doesn't mean yours wasn't greatly missed." She looked around the room, at all of Giovanni's grandchildren. "And I see there has been a great deal in yours."

"Yes, there has been. But I never released the love I have for you. I simply made room for more."

"I think we have a great deal to discuss, Bartolo," Lucia said. "Don't you?"

"Yes. I think we do."

He looped his arm around hers, and the two of them made their way slowly out of the room. The siblings looked at one another and, for once, no one seemed to know what to say.

But it was a strange thing, the realization that they were all in the same room. Nate included. They were all here together, united by their grandfather's quest to bring closure to the long-ago love affair.

If Alex were a sentimental man at all, he might even say that love had brought them together.

Gabriella would say that. Probably the moment they were alone.

It was a strange thing to him that he felt he could anticipate the sort of thing she might say. He couldn't recall ever feeling like that about anyone before. Couldn't recall ever thinking he was certain about the feelings of the person standing beside him. Though something about Gabriella felt ingrained in him, intrinsic to his system. He could guess at her thoughts, emotions and opinions as easily as he could guess at his own. Potentially easier.

"Alex," Gabriella said, "can we talk?"

It wasn't exactly what he had anticipated her saying, but she wanted to talk because she was having some kind of reaction to the scene between their grandparents. And that he had figured out. For some reason, he drew comfort in his ability to recognize and anticipate Gabriella's moods. Which wouldn't matter at all when she went back to Aceena. Not at all. It wasn't as though they would keep in touch. Wasn't as though they would exchange fluffy texts with emoticons like modern-day star-crossed lovers.

"Of course," he said, placing his hand on the small of her back and leading her from the room, ignoring the questioning gazes of his siblings as they followed their progress.

"Gardens?" she asked.

"Not a gallery?"

"I like gardens. And galleries. And libraries. I contain multitudes."

He laughed. "Yes, you do. You are large indeed. In a very small way."

She inclined her head, smiling at him. Her expression was impish, but there was something serious behind her dark eyes, and it filled him with a sense of foreboding. Yet another ridiculous thing, because there was nothing that Gabriella could possibly say to him that was worth feeling a sense of foreboding over. He had never felt foreboding in his life.

"This way," he said, leading her down the long corridor that would take them to the back doors and out to the garden. "I'm not sure it's as spectacular as the grounds in Aceena. But they'll have to do." He pushed the French doors open, then stood like a footman, his hand outstretched, indicating that Gabriella should go ahead of him. She did. And he took great joy in watching her walk out into the sunshine, the rays of the sun shining over the glossy dark waves of her hair. She was a bright, shiny, beautiful thing, a thing that he could not hope to possess. Not with all of the money that he had in his bank account. Not with all the power and influence he wielded. Because it would take something else to hold on to a woman like Gabriella, something he simply didn't have. Something he couldn't even identify. And if he couldn't identify it, how could he hope to obtain it?

This was a foolish line of thinking. He was fine. He had been fine until his grandfather had sent him on the fool's errand to collect the painting. This was Giovanni's happy ending, at ninety-eight, and it had nothing at all to do with Alex. Alex would go back to the way things were. Alex would go back to life without Gabby. That was as it should be. And he should want nothing else.

She walked over to a stone bench that was positioned just in front of a manicured hedge and took a seat, drawing one delicate, manicured finger over the hard, cold surface. Then she looked up at him. "It's a very sad thing that our grandparents had to wait half a century to find each other again."

"But a very happy thing that they have each other again, yes?"

"Yes. It is very happy."

"And as they both said, they did not lack for love in their lives."

"Yes. You're right. But don't you think…considering what they said, considering the evidence…that they never forgot each other? That their feelings for each other never lessened? That what they shared was different? They reserved a special place inside of them that was never replaced by anyone else. Not by the people they married, not by their children, not by their grandchildren. I believe that they both had happy lives. But I also believe that what they shared between each other was unique. I believe that it was special in a way that nothing else was. And I believe—"

She swallowed hard, looking up at the sky, curling her fingers around the edge of the bench and planting her feet firmly on the ground.

"I believe that there is such a thing as true love. Real love. The kind that people write sonnets about, the kind that makes people paint. That makes them sing. Like a real 'I have one half of the magic amulet, and you have the other half and they can only be complete when they're together' kind of love. I just saw it in there."

He felt cold inside. And it had nothing to do with the clear, frostbitten December day, and everything to do with the words that were spilling out of Gabriella's mouth.

"What is the point to all of this, Gabriella?"

"I think…I think that we might have that. Because it doesn't make sense, Alex. None of this makes sense. We don't. We should have nothing in common. Nothing to talk about. Attraction might be one thing, sexual compatibility another. But there's more than that. I have never felt more like myself than when I'm with you. I thought, all this time, that I needed to find someone who is like me. That I needed to find someone who would keep me safe, the way I had kept myself safe. But that isn't it at all. I don't want to be safe. I want to be with you." She laughed. "I guess it doesn't really sound right. It isn't like I think you're going to put me in danger…"

"No," he said, the word coming out of his mouth, heart tortured. "You are exactly right. I am going to put you in danger. I already have. It's evidenced by the fact that we're having this conversation. You should not feel these things for me, Gabby. I made it very clear that what we had was physical, and only physical."

"Yes," she said, her voice sounding hollow, as though he had already eviscerated something essential inside of her. "I know you did. Then things changed for me. I thought it wasn't entirely impossible that they had changed for you."

"And that is where our differences are a problem. You are innocent. And for you, all of this is new. So of course things have changed. And I can understand why you might have thought they would change for me. But you have to understand that nothing about this is original to me," he said, directly combating his earlier thoughts. Because he needed to. For himself, not just for her. "I have conducted more of these relationships than I can count. And there is absolutely nothing unique about you."

She blinked furiously, tears glittering in her beautiful eyes, and he wanted nothing more than to wipe them away. But he had put them there, so he forfeited the right. "But you didn't… If I wasn't different, then you would have had me the moment you wanted me. I don't think you would have held me on the floor of the library and used your words to—"

"That's the thing, Gabby, you don't think, because you don't have any idea how this works. When a man wants to seduce a woman he appeals to her in any way he can. I'm not above pretending to be a much nicer man than I am. I was seemingly honest with you," he said, the words cutting his throat on their way out. "I told you about my fearsome reputation, but then I treated you gently. I made you feel like you were different. What better way to seduce a virgin? But I never wanted your love, darling girl. I only wanted your body."

"Why are you saying this?"

"Because it is time I told the truth. The moment you started spouting poetry I knew this had to be over. It was one thing when I thought you were going to quietly return to your home country the moment the painting was delivered. Clearly, you had other designs. And I don't have any interest in prolonging this farce."

She closed her eyes, a single tear trailing down her cheek. "That wasn't the farce. *This* is."

"Gabriella," he said, his voice hardened, harsh. "I told you the sort of man I am. I deal in business. In exchanges. We exchanged pleasure. That's all there is for me. Beyond that? I kept my own brother a secret to try and protect the reputation of my father. A man who was debauched beyond reason. That's the sort of thing I stand in defense of."

"No. You say that. You're determined to make sure that I and everyone else think you're a monster. Why? What are you hiding?" She opened her eyes, meeting his gaze directly, and anger was replacing the sadness that had been there only a moment ago.

"That," he said, "is my deepest, darkest secret, *cara mia*. I am hiding nothing. The water is just as shallow as it appears from the surface. Nothing is running deep here."

"I understand that you need to believe that, Alex. I understand that it's what you need everyone else to believe. What I don't understand is why."

He spread his hands. "There is nothing to understand. That is the simple, tragic truth of me. My legend is far more interesting than I will ever be. Stories of me being a monster. Of being heartless, and cruel. The simple fact is I'm self-serving. There is nothing intricate to figure out. I do what makes me money. I do what brings me pleasure. Those are my motivations. Those are my actions. Women, the media, they like to pretend that there is something else beneath all of that. I am no more interesting than my father and mother ever were."

"No," she said, her voice a whisper. "You said you didn't want to be like him."

"I said a lot of things. Don't believe them. I believe this. It's over, Gabriella. The painting is delivered, our grandparents are reunited. They can keep their true love. I will keep my money, my varied sex life and my freedom. You can go back to your books."

"Alex," she said, her voice broken, a plea.

It stabbed him, made him feel like he was being scraped raw from the inside out. This was for the best. He had to end it. He had to end it with the kind of finality his grandfather had ended things with Lucia. But he would leave no painting behind. He would leave no trail of bread crumbs for Gabriella to find her way back to him eventually.

What he did, he did for her best interests. For her future. She really would find a man who was better than him. She thought, right now, that he was more exciting than the intellectual, nice man that she would ultimately end up with, but in the future she would see that she was wrong. She would understand that she needed someone companionable, someone stable, someone who would give her everything that she deserved and more.

She was emotionally scarred by parents who had been so much like his own. And he would do nothing to continue that scarring. To continue that pain. Removing himself now was the kindest thing, even though it didn't seem like it now.

"You were right," he said, knowing that the death knell to all of this was on his lips even now. "The rake never ends up with the wallflower. He crosses the room for her, Gabby, every time. Because she's needy. Because she's vulnerable. Because she's a challenge, a change in flavor to a jaded palate. But he doesn't end up with her. He doesn't end up with anyone."

And then he turned, leaving her standing in the garden, leaving her breaking to pieces behind him, while his own chest did the same.

It was so very like Giovanni and Lucia. But with one major difference. There would never be a time in Alex's life when he stood in a roomful of his grandchildren and told this story. Because there would be no grandchildren for him. There would be no other woman, no wife.

It would be up to his brothers and sisters to carry on the bloodline, because he would not.

He would leave nothing behind. Not his tainted blood, not any Lost Mistresses.

Without him, Gabriella would be free to have love in her life. She would not hold on to him.

He wasn't worth it.

CHAPTER FOURTEEN

GABRIELLA WAS IN a daze. She had been ever since Alex had left her sitting out in the garden at his grandfather's estate. Now, she was staying at the estate. She had stumbled into the house some two hours later and found her grandmother, who was of course planning on staying and reacquainting herself with Giovanni, and spending as much time with him as possible with the remaining time he had.

She should feel happy for them. Part of her did feel happy for them. But so much of her was broken, smashed into tiny pieces. Tiny, aching pieces. That made it difficult to feel wholly happy for anyone or anything.

She wasn't entirely certain she would ever take a full breath again, much less crack a full smile.

It was seriously dramatic, but she felt seriously dramatic.

She would like to think of Alex as her first love. Her first heartbreak. But with each and every beat of her heart the word wasn't *first*, it was *only*. Her only love. Her only lover. The only man she would ever want, the only man she could ever possibly need.

She was hurt. But she was also angry at him. Because no matter what he said she knew that there was more to him than this. She knew that he hadn't seduced her, tricked her, just for a little bit of sport. He felt something for her, and she knew that. The fact that he was so cruel when he'd abandoned her earlier today was proof enough of that.

He talked about being like his father, but she knew that people like their parents were not intentionally cruel. They were simply self-seeking. When he had been confronted with his half brother he had preferred to ignore the situation.

This was different. His reaction was different. Yes, she knew he had a reputation for being a monster, but she had also never seen it in action.

Still, even knowing that something deeper was going on inside of Alex, it didn't mean this didn't hurt. Because while she had confidence that he had feelings for her that went beyond the physical, she had no confidence that they would be able to resolve it.

Though there was something wonderful in finding a belief in true love because of the reunion of their grandparents, there was also something sobering about the fact that it had taken them more than fifty years to come and find each other. She didn't want to wait fifty years for Alex.

She flopped backward onto the bed, groaning loudly. She closed her eyes, letting her lips part, imagining that Alex was here. That he was leaning in, about to kiss them. She let her imagination drift. To the way that he touched her. The way that he held her.

She might have been a virgin, but she wasn't an idiot.

She opened her eyes, sighing heavily.

There was a knock on the door and Gabriella rolled onto her side, her head on her arm. "Come in," she said, not quite sure why she was allowing anyone entry when she felt like day-old crusty bread.

When the door opened, Gabriella straightened. It was her grandmother. "Hello, Gabriella," the older woman said, walking into the room slowly.

"I trust everything is going well?"

Lucia smiled. "Better than."

"I'm glad."

"I know Bartolo's health is not as good as it might be, but I am more than happy to devote time to caring for him."

Those words, so gentle, so serene, shook something inside of Gabriella. It made her think of Alex again. She would do that for him. She would care for him. She didn't need the whole world in return; she only needed what he could give. At least for now. If he hadn't sent her away she would be willing to be patient. She didn't need him to throw rope around the moon and lasso it, didn't need him to pull it down for her. He was the moon all by himself. The idiot.

"Gabriella," her grandmother said, her tone gentler now. "Is there something you wish to tell me?"

"Alex," she said, because she knew that would be enough.

"I did warn you," the older woman said, her eyes soft, no condemnation in her voice.

"I know you did. Unfortunately, Alessandro was a bit more persuasive than you are."

Lucia laughed then. "They always are. I have some experience with that, as you may know."

"Yes. I know."

"And sometimes they push us away because they think they are doing what's best for us. In truth, while I know Bartolo believes I was angry at him, I was angry at myself. I knew what he was doing that whole time. He was trying to play the part of nobleman. He didn't want me to be denied anything he considered my birthright. Didn't want me disowned by my family. But I have always felt that I should have fought harder. Always wondered what would have happened if I would have told him no. If I would never have let him get away with hurting me to save me."

The truth of her grandmother's words resonated inside of her. Because it was what she had imagined Alex might be doing. Of course, she was too afraid to hope. Maybe he simply didn't want to be with her. "How do you know?"

Her grandmother took a step forward, patting her on the hand. "You don't. Not unless you go ask. Take it from someone who spent half a century wishing she would have asked—it's worth the risk. Pride does not keep you warm at night. Pride won't smile at you every morning, day in day out, with ever deepening lines as the years pass. Pride is very cold comfort, Gabriella."

Lucia straightened and walked back out of the room, closing the door softly behind her. Gabriella thought of the way Alex had looked at her before leaving her in the garden earlier. Of the painful words he'd spoken, designed specifically to inflict the deepest wounds on her.

Her grandmother was right. There was no room for pride. Her pride could go straight to hell, but she would keep her love for Alex.

She had spent a great many years hiding. Trying to prevent herself from being rejected ever again, the way her parents made her feel rejected. But all that had ever gotten her was a dusty library. She was done with that. She would have her dusty library and her man.

It was suddenly clear. She'd been doing her family's genealogy for years. Trying to uncover the mysteries of the past, to shine a light on history and events lived by other people. She used it to hide.

But there would be no more hiding. She could no longer pin everything on the past. She had to make her own life. Her own history.

She stood up, vibrating with determination. Alessandro Di Sione might think he was the most fearsome creature to roam the earth. But hell had no fury like Gabriella D'Oro when she was scorned. And she was determined to show him that.

CHAPTER FIFTEEN

ALEX WAS CONTEMPLATING the merit of filling his bathtub with whiskey and seeing if he could absorb the alcohol straight through his skin. Anything to dull the roar of pain that was writhing through his body, the pounding in his temples, the bone-deep ache that had settled down beneath his skin and wrapped itself around his entire being.

Drinking had proven ineffective. It wasn't strong enough. He could still see her face. Could still see the way she looked at him. Wounded, impossibly hurt, as he had done what he had thought to be the noble thing.

Was it the noble thing? Or are you simply a coward?

That question had been rattling around in his brain for hours, settling like acid in his gut and eating away at his every justification.

And once it had been introduced, he couldn't shake it. Was he protecting her? Or was he protecting himself? She had been very open about the fact that she had hidden away from the world, choosing to protect herself from further rejection because of the way her parents had treated her. Like an incidental. Like she didn't matter.

And he had…

Hadn't he hidden away from the world, too? Behind the facade of being a dragon, of being a soulless monster. Keeping everyone at a distance. Most especially the half brother who had been there that terrible night. Who had been wound around that most painful event.

The thought was enough to take his breath away. To realize that his own actions had been born not of a need to keep control, but out of fear. It ate away at the very foundation of who he believed he was. He thought himself strong. He thought himself in total command.

Now he wondered if he was still a boy, hiding from difficult feelings. Difficult decisions. Concealing the existence of the truth so that he didn't have to face it. Just as he had done with Nate.

But what life could she have with him? What did he offer to Gabriella? He knew what she did for him. She gave him hope. She made him see art, made him see beauty. With her, he experienced softness, hope, in a way that he hadn't done in his entire life. Yes, he knew exactly what she offered him, and he feared that all he had to offer her was his endless, dark well of neediness. Left open the night his parents died. It held nothing but fear, nothing but anguish, and those things consumed, they didn't give.

Suddenly, the door to his apartment swung open.

He had to wonder for a moment just how much he'd had to drink, because there stood Gabriella, the light from the hallway illuminating her with a golden halo around her dark hair, making her look like an angel standing in the middle of hell. His own personal hell. As though she had come to raise him from perdition.

And he desperately wanted it to be so.

How was it that this young innocent could reduce the jaded playboy like himself to such a needy, desperate thing? How was it that she had reached inside of him and scraped him raw? He should have had all the control here. She should be the one in pain because he had ended things. And he should be able to move on as he had always done. And yet, he couldn't.

"Gabby," he said, the word raw and rough as his insides.

"You don't get to call me that," she said, sweeping into the room and slamming the door behind her. "Not unless you intend to fix what you did."

"My list of sins is long, Gabriella. You have to be more specific."

"The small matter of lying to me and breaking my heart." She crossed her arms, her proud chin tilted upward, her small frame vibrating with rage. "I understand. It took me a while, because I had to dig beneath my own pain to understand, but I do. You're afraid. Just like me. And just like me you are protecting yourself."

Hearing the words from Gabriella's lips made it even harder for him to deny. He had suspicions about his own behavior, but they were just that—suspicions.

Gabriella knew him. And he trusted that. She had an intelligence about emotions, the kind that he could hardly lay claim to.

"But we can't do that anymore," she said. "It isn't worth it. What do we get for it? Years of wishing we were together? We can be what we're expected to be. We can be safe. No, Alex, I shouldn't be with you. I'm a princess. And I should be with a man who is at the very least a member of nobility, or failing that, not a complete and total dissolute playboy. You should be with a woman who is sophisticated, who has a tough outer shell and a lot more experience than I have. But that is what we want. We want each other. Because you're my deep love, Alex. The other half of my amulet. The one that I'll never forget. You are the hole in my soul, the one that I have carried from the day I was born and I wasn't even aware that it was there until the moment I met you."

Her words echoed inside him, rang with truth. It was the same for him. He knew it was the same for him.

"How?" He swallowed hard. "How do we just forget everything else?"

"I figure it's either that or we forget that we love each other, Alex. And I would so much rather forget my pain. I would so much rather forget my fear. I would rather forget that on paper we don't make any sense and just remember that I love you. In the end, doesn't that sound easier?"

His chest seized tight, his breathing becoming labored. "I'm not sure if there's anything simple about love, Gabriella."

"Maybe not. Maybe I'm living in a fantasy. But… Oh, Alex, how I would love to live in this fantasy with you. I know you think I'm young and silly—"

"No," he said. "I don't think you're silly. I think you are magically unspoiled by all of the things that have happened to you in your life. I think you are a gift that your parents didn't deserve, that they didn't appreciate. I think that you are a gift I don't deserve."

"Well, what's the use in being a gift that no one wants?"

He felt like his chest was going to crack open. "I do want you. I do. But…I am…a thousand years too old for you. A thousand ways too corrupt. Wouldn't you rather be with a different man?"

"No," she said, the word so simple, with no hesitation. "No one else made me want to come out of the library. I liked small things. Quiet things. And what I feel for you…it isn't quiet or small. It's big and loud and it rings in my ears, in my chest, and it terrifies me. But I want it still. I was so caught up in the fact that the rake could come after the wallflower that I didn't stop to think how amazing it was that I came out of hiding for you. Alex, the fact that I want you is a miracle in and of itself. I'm not sure you appreciate that."

He laughed, but there was no humor in the sound. "Believe me, I do."

"Well, so do I. I love you. And I'm sorry if that isn't sophisticated. I'm sorry if it wasn't supposed to happen. But it did. And it's the most amazing, wonderful thing. So much better than hiding away. Please, come with me. Away from the guilt. Because I know you still feel guilty. But you were a boy. You have to forgive yourself."

He nodded slowly. "I do. Because you're right, I was a boy. But I'm not a boy now. I'm a man. Still, I was hiding like one. And it has to stop, Gabriella. You are right. I was very dedicated to the idea that I was a monster. Convincing you, to convince myself. Because I'm a very convenient hiding place. That mask was the best thing I had. It kept everyone away. But…I don't want that anymore. I thought that it made me strong. I convinced myself that I was turning away from the way my parents lived. Cutting myself off from that kind of reckless behavior, keeping myself from poisoning other people in my life. But I wasn't afraid for others. I was afraid for myself. But you are right. Living without you would be far worse than learning to let go of all this."

He took a step toward her, cupping the back of her head and gazing down into her dark eyes. "If you will have me, after all the things I said, after everything I have done, both before and since I met you, then I would be very honored if you would… I suppose I can ask you to marry me, can I?"

"No," she said, causing his heart to sink. "You can't. Because you haven't said you love me yet."

"I thought that was implied."

"Not good enough. I like art, I like poetry, I like books. I like all of the beauty laid out before me."

He felt a smile curve his lips upward. "My face isn't enough?"

"It's a start. But I need the words."

"I love you, beautiful Gabby."

"Really?" she asked, tears filling her eyes. The good kind of tears. The kind that made his chest ache and his whole body shake at the wonder of it. "Even though I'm not boring?"

"Most especially because you aren't boring. Because you are clever. Because you teach me things—about the world and about myself. I want to spend the rest of my life holding you, touching you, being with you. I want your lips to be the last lips I ever kiss. And your heart to be the only one I ever hold. And in case you missed it the first time, I love you."

She smiled, the kind of dreamy smile he had never dared hope to be on the receiving end of. The kind of dreamy smile he hadn't even known he ever wanted to be on the receiving end of. Amazing the things that his princess was teaching him. "That's better."

"Now can I propose to you?"

"You really want to get married, Alex?"

"Yes. Because that's what you deserve. Forever. All in. And…I still feel like there are things inside of me that I'll have to work through. I'm afraid that I'll take too much from you."

"Never. Maybe you will sometimes. But then, there will be other times when I take too much from you. We're not in half-and-half. We are all in. Forever. When you need to be carried, Alex, I'll carry you," she said, taking a step forward and resting her palm on his cheek. "And I know that when I need to be carried you'll carry me. That's what love is. It gives. We know what it looks like when people take, when they consume and do only what pleases them. But that isn't us. It isn't this."

"If I falter, Gabriella," he said, grabbing hold of her chin with his thumb and forefinger, "promise me you'll put me back on the path."

"You have my word."

"I can't paint you, Gabriella. I can't show you the way that I see you. I can't explain it to you in terms of art, and really, I'm not all that good with poetry."

"Lies. You're wonderful with it."

"I'm really not. So I'll just say it plain, and honest. I love you. From now until forever."

"That's really all I need."

"No white tigers?"

She tapped her chin, as though she were considering it. "I wouldn't say no to a white tiger."

"Well," he said, "I may not be able to accommodate you there. But how about a white Christmas wedding?"

She smiled, throwing her arms around his neck and stretching up on her tiptoes to give him a kiss. "That sounds just about perfect."

EPILOGUE

A WEDDING BETWEEN a billionaire and a princess really was an amazing thing. Mostly because when titles and money were thrown around it became surprisingly easy to throw things together in only a couple of weeks.

The entire family came to help Gabriella and Alessandro celebrate their love. Love was always beautiful, but there was something particularly beautiful about watching Gabriella and Alessandro joined together. It wasn't simply the ring she wore on her finger, or the tiara she wore in her dark hair, nor was it the earrings that glittered in her ears. It was the love that radiated between them, the strange sort of symmetry evident there.

Giovanni had to wonder if their family blood was simply destined to love a D'Oro. If there was something ingrained on a soul-deep level that was inescapable. If so, he was glad of that. As he sat, watching his beloved eldest grandson pledge his life to the granddaughter of the woman he had always loved, he felt a sense of absolute completion wash through him.

Though he imagined that had something to do with

the woman sitting at his side. Queen Lucia, his true lost mistress, finally returned to him. It was a miracle.

And it didn't matter how many years he had left to his name, because he knew they would be the happiest years yet. And he imagined there were very few people who could claim such a thing.

At his appointment last week the doctors had told him he was doing well, something no one had ever expected to happen at his age. They also told him he was healthier than should be possible. That he was a miracle. He wasn't entirely certain that he was a miracle, but there were certainly miracles all around him. Each and every one of his grandchildren, settled and fallen in love. Nate, brought into the family in a real and true way. Alessandro healed from the wounds left behind by his parents.

And Lucia by his side.

Yes, as he looked around the family estate, lushly decorated for Christmas, glittering with lights, ribbon and boughs of holly, he couldn't help but think that the miracle had nothing to do with him at all.

The miracle was, and had always been, love, available for anyone who would reach out and take it.

And though it was late in his life, he was taking it now.

He took Lucia's hand in his, just as Alessandro pulled Gabriella into his arms for a kiss. He looked at Lucia and saw that her eyes were fixed to the painting hanging in the great room. Perhaps scandalous in some ways, but then, when it came to the Di Sione family, it was difficult to say what was scandalous and what was simply everyday business.

"I love you," he said, squeezing Lucia's hand.

She took her eyes away from the painting and looked back at him, offering a slow smile.

"I can see that. I can see it clearly."

* * * * *

If you enjoyed the stunning conclusion to
THE BILLIONAIRE'S LEGACY
catch up with the previous titles:

DI SIONE'S INNOCENT CONQUEST
by Carol Marinelli
THE DI SIONE SECRET BABY
by Maya Blake
TO BLACKMAIL A DI SIONE
by Rachael Thomas
THE RETURN OF THE DI SIONE WIFE
by Caitlin Crews
DI SIONE'S VIRGIN MISTRESS
by Sharon Kendrick
A DI SIONE FOR THE GREEK'S PLEASURE
by Kate Hewitt
A DEAL FOR THE DI SIONE RING
by Jennifer Hayward

#3509 PURSUED BY THE DESERT PRINCE

The Sauveterre Siblings

by Dani Collins

When Prince Kasim finds he's falsely accused Angelique Sauveterre of an affair with his future brother-in-law, he can't resist this feisty beauty himself! Angelique blossoms under Kasim's touch and surrenders. But can he give her more than passion and precious jewels?

#3510 THE TEMPORARY MRS. MARCHETTI

by Melanie Milburne

Cristiano Marchetti proposes to Alice Piper to fulfill the conditions of a will. But his real agenda is revenge—for leaving him years ago! That is until it seems the future Mrs. Marchetti might become more than Cristiano's *temporary* bride...

#3511 THE SICILIAN'S DEFIANT VIRGIN

by Susan Stephens

Luca Tebaldi is furious at Jennifer Sanderson for inheriting his brother's estate—he'll seduce the truth out of her! But this sensual innocent sets Luca's senses on fire, forcing him to confront what *she* is enticing out of *him*!

#3512 THE FORGOTTEN GALLO BRIDE

by Natalie Anderson

Zara Falconer's wedding to Tomas Gallo set her free, but an accident wiped Tomas's memory before he could annul their vows. When she discovers this tortured man is still her husband, she has to ask—will their passion bring back Tomas's memories?

Somehow Lydia was back against the wall with Raul's hands on either side of her head.

She put her hands up to his chest and felt him solid beneath her palms and she just felt him there a moment and then looked up to his eyes.

His mouth moved in close and as it did she stared right into his eyes.

She could feel heat hover between their mouths in a slow tease before they first met.

Then they met.

And all that had been missing was suddenly there.

Yet the gentle pressure his mouth exerted, though blissful, caused a flood of sensations until the gentleness of his kiss was no longer enough.

A slight inhale, a hitch in her breath and her lips parted, just a little, and he slipped his tongue in.

The moan she made went straight to his groin.

At first taste she was his and he knew it for her hands moved to the back of his head and he kissed her as hard as her fingers demanded.

More so even.

His tongue was wicked and her fingers tightened in his thick hair and she could feel the wall cold and hard against her shoulders.

It was the middle of Rome just after six and even down a side street there was no real hiding from the crowds.

Lydia didn't care.

He slid one arm around her waist to move her body away from the wall and closer into his, so that her head could fall backward.

If there was a bed, she would be on it.

If there was a room, they would close the door.

Yet there wasn't and so he halted them, but only their lips.

Their bodies were heated and close and he looked her right in the eye. His mouth was wet from hers and his hair a little messed from her fingers.

"What do you want to do?" Raul asked while knowing it was a no-brainer, and he went for her neck.

She had never thought that a kiss beneath her ear could make it so impossible to breathe let alone think.

"What do you want to do?" He whispered to her skin and blew on her neck, damp from his kisses, and then he raised his head and met her eye. "Tonight I can give you anything you want."

HPEXP0217